From Meaning to Desire

To Graham and Elizabeth,

Have a good read.

Love,
Doug

From Meaning to Desire

Douglas Uzzell

Copyright © 2013 by Douglas Uzzell.

Library of Congress Control Number:		2013905192
ISBN:	Hardcover	978-1-4836-1300-0
	Softcover	978-1-4836-1299-7
	Ebook	978-1-4836-1301-7

All rights reserved. No part of this book may be reproduced or transmitted in any form or by any means, electronic or mechanical, including photocopying, recording, or by any information storage and retrieval system, without permission in writing from the copyright owner.

This is a work of fiction. Names, characters, places and incidents either are the product of the author's imagination or are used fictitiously, and any resemblance to any actual persons, living or dead, events, or locales is entirely coincidental.

This book was printed in the United States of America.

Rev. date: 04/22/2013

To order additional copies of this book, contact:
Xlibris Corporation
1-888-795-4274
www.Xlibris.com
Orders@Xlibris.com
127440

Contents

Epigraphs 9

PART ONE
A DOUBLE SELF

Lillian at Thirty-eight 17
Crashing and Burning 28

PART TWO
THE MAKING OF AN ALLIGATOR WRESTLER

A Counterfeit Cajun 41
Alligator Hides 53

PART THREE
FITTING IN

Civil Disobedience 65
Backlash 78

PART FOUR
JOINING

Doing Business 99
Invisibility 115

PART FIVE
RESURRECTIONS OF MARLOW

Resurrections of Marlow 141

Dedication

To Linda,

and to Shawn, Gwendolyn, and Caitlin:

my love and deepest thanks to each of you.

Dedication

To Linda,

and to Shawn, Gwendolyn, and Caitlin:

my love and deepest thanks to each of you.

EPIGRAPHS

The world does not come to us prepackaged with determinate objects with their determinate properties. Instead, we have to learn the meaning of physical objects, which we do by watching them, handling them, subjecting them to forces, and seeing how they can be used—in short, by forms of interactive inquiry that are at once bodily and reflective.[1]

—Mark Johnson, *The Meaning of the Body*

A noiseless, patient spider,
I mark'd, where, on a little promontory, it stood, isolated;
Mark'd how, to explore the vacant, vast surrounding,
It launch'd forth filament, filament, filament, out of itself;
Ever unreeling them—ever tirelessly speeding them.

And you, O my Soul, where you stand,
Surrounded, surrounded, in measureless oceans of space,
Ceaselessly musing, venturing, throwing,—seeking the spheres, to connect them;
Till the bridge you will need, be form'd—till the ductile anchor hold;
Till the gossamer thread you fling, catch somewhere, O my Soul.[2]

—Walt Whitman, *Leaves of Grass*

[1.] Mark Johnson, *The Meaning of the Body: Aesthetics of Human Understanding* (Chicago: The University of Chicago Press, 2007), 46.
[2.] Walt Whitman, *Leaves of Grass* (New York: Bantam Dell, 2004), 488.

PREFACE

The stories that follow are works of fiction, and the characters in them are imaginary, having lived in my brain for upward of fifty years. The first eight are set in western Louisiana during the part of the long civil rights struggle that was intensifying during 1960. Though public events, such as protest demonstrations and reactions against them, did take place in Louisiana in 1960, there is no intentional correspondence between the fictional events described in the stories and the real, often more violent, events that occurred outside my imagination. Actual physical landmarks are woven through the narratives only in the interest of verisimilitude. The "human" characters whose stories are told are intended to be lifelike, but not alive. Any resemblances between them and persons living or dead are purely unintentional and coincidental.

That is true also for the ninth story, "Resurrections of Marlow," except that the colonial violence that energizes *its* action—though traceable to the same fifteenth-century European continental breakout that eventuated in the North American civil rights movement—is here more narrowly situated among South Vietnamese peasants seven years later. The title character was born and raised in southwestern Louisiana and appears in some of the Red River stories so that the arc of his life from North America to Southeast Asia (and implicitly, back) indirectly reveals something of the scope and texture of the five-hundred-year trajectory of the great European colonial adventure, at least as a kind of antistrophe in its grisly colonial performance.

Acknowledgment

Cover photograph courtesy of Colin McWilliams

Part One
A Double Self

The self is, at the very least, double: one self to think with and one to think about. Beyond that, there is the uncanniness of an imagined future and a remembered past. And beyond that, of an imagined past and a remembered future: the confusions of the life of fantasy and desire.[3]

—Avivah Gottlieb Zornberg, *The Murmuring Deep*

---

[3] Avivah Gottlieb Zornberg, *The Murmuring Deep* (New York: Schoken Books, 2009), 16.

Lillian at Thirty-Eight

Depression is a self-cure for the terrors of aliveness, of being alive to one's losses and therefore to one's desires.[4]

—Adam Phillips, *On Flirtation*

"What's their address?" Gerald asked, craning his neck to see through the windshield.

The flow of brackish Gulf air through the car's wing vents had slowed. Miraculously, the address was still in the glove compartment, where she remembered having put it. Lillian laughed. Gerald smiled quizzically.

"I was just thinking," she explained, controlling the urge to continue laughing, "what a pair we are: our only child a third of the way across the country and we don't even know her address."

The smile evaporated from Gerald's face. Lillian's urge to laugh persisted; but as they began looking for street signs, saliva flooded her mouth, leaving her struggling to swallow fast enough, fending off nausea. At the slower speed, she felt perspiration forming on her face and back.

"Gerald," she said, "please let's stay at an air-conditioned motel, no matter what the kids say?"

Gerald frowned cautiously. "But they're expecting us to stay with them."

She shook her head, flushed and winded. "I just don't want to. It just doesn't feel right."

"I don't know, Lillian," Gerald said. "That seems so . . ."

Her panic passed, and she was not surprised to hear herself as though from far away, saying, "You're probably right."

"But I don't want you to feel . . ."

[4.] Adam Phillips, *On Flirtation* (Cambridge, Mass.: Harvard University Press, 1994), 82.

"No, that's fine. I'm fine." She touched his arm and dropped her voice. "Just a passing impulse," she added. "Okay?"

They turned off the main road onto a narrow street topped with crushed shells. To their right, the Gulf was visible between the houses, strewn along a perilously narrow beach.

"Must be high tide," Gerald observed.

"I should hope it doesn't come up any farther!" Lillian exclaimed.

Gerald glanced at her covertly as she turned her head away. Seawater had always reminded her of living soup. A slight reflux brought to her throat a remembrance of last night's rum and coffee.

Gerald parked the car in front of a white stilt house. A pickup truck with the name of the University of Florida stenciled on the side stood beside the house. Lillian stepped out of the car into the bright sunlight, holding on to the door handle for a moment until she found her balance, welcoming the heat of the metal on the palm of her hand.

A clothesline ran from somewhere behind the house to a pole ten feet to the side. Diapers flapped from the line. Lillian and Gerald stood gazing, like two children just abandoned on a new planet. The open space beneath the house had been enclosed with softly undulating bamboo shades. Cindy had written that Robert stores fish tanks below the house and that he uses them in his doctoral research. Beyond that, Lillian knew almost nothing about Robert, his work, or the young couple's life together.

"The adjective 'quaint' comes to mind," Lillian muttered. "Or the noun phrase 'Pooh Corner,' maybe." Again she resists the urge to laugh.

"It's a cute little place," Gerald said, chuckling much more positively, missing her tone or ignoring it. "Right on the water too," he added. "I'll bet Robert loves it."

Lillian formed her mouth into what she hoped resembled a smile. The house looked vulnerable to her, almost pathetic, with its spindly supports rising from the sand beach, the bamboo shades breathing the sultry wind.

To Lillian's dismay, the scene's composition began to fall apart. Outside her visual range, the sound of Gerald's voice had turned tinny and distant, like a record playing on a neighbor child's phonograph. She closed her eyes against the delusion, and when she opened them again, the surroundings had returned to normal. Gerald examined her face quizzically. Sighing, he started around the side of the house; and after a brief hesitation, she followed him, stepping carefully, trying to keep the sand out of her shoes. The two of them made their way up a steep outside stairway with a door at the top. Ignoring the buzzer, Gerald tapped lightly on the door. "Baby might be sleeping," he whispered.

They waited while heavy footfalls shook the building. A bearded young man threw open the door and greeted them. "Dad!" he cried, pawing at Gerald's shoulder. "Mom! How are you?" Lillian winced but managed a smile.

Gerald addressed Robert gleefully as "Big Guy" and demanded to be shown his "two gorgeous females."

Behind Robert, Lillian could see Cindy beaming at her father, kissing his cheek with a loudly vocalized "muuummph!"

At that very moment, Robert kissed Lillian smack on the mouth, startling her. She resisted the urge to wipe her mouth, imagining that she still felt his saliva. Cindy disengaged from Gerald and gave Lillian a warm smile.

"Mother," she murmured as they brushed cheeks, and Cindy stepped back.

"Come, look," she cried, suddenly breaking from her mother with fresh energy and pulling both parents by the hand down a short hallway into a bedroom. At the foot of the bed was a crib, and in it, a sleeping infant. "Meet Emily!" Cindy whispered, looking from Gerald to Lillian with brimming eyes. Venetian blinds and chintz curtains darkened the scene, and two floor fans supplemented the Gulf breeze. Compared to the outside, the bedroom was cool and peaceful. As if on cue, the baby began to fret and squirm, dissolving the image.

"Uh oh," Gerald whispered.

"No, that's fine," Cindy replied in a normal voice. "She needs to get up now, so she'll sleep tonight." The baby opened her slowly focusing eyes and grimaced.

"Oh, you dear, dear little one," Gerald cried in a hushed voice. Lillian looked curiously at him, abashedly envious of his line and delivery. Her mouth could never have formed those words with his sincerity.

The baby whimpered. "Oh my," Gerald protested.

Unexpectedly, Robert crooned a condescension, "Oh goodness, goodness. Her so sad and hungry and maybe wet. Poor, poor baby."

Lillian averted her eyes to hide her irritation at his tone but noticed that Cindy had caught her expression. Lillian wondered what it would feel like to call this man "son-in-law" or "husband" for that matter.

Interrupting the ceremony, Cindy lifted the infant to her shoulder and murmured to quiet her. With impressive economy of motion, she picked a fresh diaper from a stack on the changing table, removed the wet diaper, sponged and powdered the baby's groin and buttocks, pinned the fresh diaper into place, dropped the wet one into the diaper pail, and with a smiling flourish, scooped up the baby again and presented her, freshly diapered, for Gerald to hold. Lillian suppressed an urge to applaud.

With the same graceful nonchalance, Cindy sat on the couch in the living room, draped a towel over her shoulder, and took the baby from Gerald. Under the towel, she offered her breast to the infant, who—smacking noisily—fell to nursing. Lillian was struck by the sure, casual grace of Cindy's movements and her freedom from embarrassment as she exposed her milk-filled breast. It was the same earthy grace Lillian had admired in European movie actresses in foreign films she had seen, though she could never imagine herself being able to move in that way, even though she could remember with pleasure the swelling of her own breasts when Cindy was a baby and even the involuntary expression of milk when the baby cried.

The other three adults in the room seemed relaxed, relishing one another's conversation, while the nursing continued. Lillian looked down on herself, sitting stiffly on the couch, wishing to participate. In a cameo flash, her own mother sat in the identical posture during her husband's wake. Lillian was so startled by the similarity and infused with the sadness of her dad's funeral that an involuntary cry escaped her lips. The other three adults looked at her. Flushing, she said, "Oh, I'm so sorry."

"For what, Mother?" Cindy asked as they continued to stare. Silence descended upon them. Like a good hostess covering a gaffe, Cindy suggested that Robert show them his fish. "He's got all kinds of aquariums and color-coded fish and everything," she said proudly, and at the same time, Lillian thought, effectively, covering her own intelligence with faux guilelessness.

Gratefully, Lillian led the way down the stairs, with Robert and Gerald following. The outside air held them in a damp caress. Muted hoots, clangs, and shuddering thuds came from a factory across the water. Fifty feet from the back of the house and down an embankment, wavelets slapped at a slender spit of sand.

Robert opened a door under the outside stairway and invited Lillian and Gerald to come in and wait while he replaced a fluorescent light bulb. The area below the residential area was floored with packed sand, enclosed by a latticework backing of the bamboo shades. All around in the gloom were flickers of light, reflections from the glass boxes. Something thumped against the wall of an aquarium on Lillian's right. The room was filled with popping bubbles and humming electric pumps, sending small trills of fear along Lillian's back.

Harsh light erupted in the room. Along all four latticework and bamboo walls, shelves rose from the sand to the raw ceiling created by the underside of plywood flooring. All the shelves were full of aquariums, most of which appeared to contain fish. In the middle of the space, four card tables were covered with bottles and equipment.

Robert laughed happily at their reaction to the fish. "Cindy thinks it's scary," he said. "She won't even come down here at night. Says it's too spooky."

Without smiling, Lillian replied, "It just feels strange to have so many living creatures in glass boxes." The two men regarded her without speaking. She wondered if they are surprised that she has a voice. Something like a wall of bulletproof glass seemed to slide between them.

Lillian moved closer to one bank of aquariums. She understood for the first time Cindy's description of the colored fish. Each vertical column of aquariums contained fish of a separate color. Around the room, there must have been twenty or thirty different bands of colors so that the three humans stood inside a living rainbow. The reality also came home to her that Cindy's life had become full, complex, and irretrievably other than her own. Lillian was surprised to feel her throat tightening against what could become tears as she was again visited by a cameo of her mother's solitary life.

Still on the other side of her imaginary glass wall, Robert was explaining to Gerald something about his project. Lillian passed the time by culling her memory for mutually pleasurable times with Cindy but was not surprised that in the mood of the moment, none came to mind, at least since Cindy had reached puberty. She wondered if Cindy ever thought of any.

"Must be the fish," she said to herself, provoking a sardonic inward grin. "Cold blooded." Just then, Gerald happened to glance her way and automatically smiled back, blessedly not realizing the meaning of her facial expression. With that, the glass wall vanished; and soon afterward, the three of them together climbed up the stairs to rejoin Cindy and the baby.

After supper, Lillian took over washing dishes—ostensibly to give Cindy time with her father and the baby, but privately to give herself a chance to work out how to get through the next few days. *Why*, she wondered, *should all this be so damned hard?* Surprised at the language of her unvoiced question, she repeated it under her breath, "damned hard, damned hard," but found herself surprisingly unperturbed.

Robert detached himself from Cindy and Gerald and offered to dry dishes. Lillian put on her "social" face and thanked him. Describing the fish downstairs as "fascinating," she asked how much longer the project would last.

"This part should be done in another month," he said, "but then I have to analyze the data and get down to writing. I hope to wrap it up in another year." He told her about a grant they are currently living on and a promised assistantship that he said should see them through until he finishes his degree and gets a more substantial job. He said that he was twenty-six—not as old as she had thought—but seven years older than Cindy (and only twelve years younger than she!). Getting used to him, Lillian found him engaging and easy to talk with. She could imagine Cindy being attracted to him. She wondered how Cindy described her to him and if she mentioned Lillian's period of problem drinking. At the thought, Lillian could feel her heart thumping in her chest.

Later, Lillian excused herself, pleading travel fatigue. Cindy showed her to the bedroom she and Gerald will share and wished her good night. Pausing, Cindy, suddenly awkward, kissed Lillian's cheek and wished her good night. Finally, she said almost shyly, "Robert and I both are glad you and Daddy are here."

Lillian thanked her, and Cindy left the room quickly. Lillian stretched out and lay quietly, listening to the others laughing and talking in the kitchen. She heard Gerald asking if there had been any racial incidents at the university, but she couldn't understand the answers. When Gerald came to bed and hugged her, she feigned sleep and pulled away out of a habit that for the moment, she regretted. She was saddened, but not surprised, when he sighed and rolled away.

She closed her eyes and did not want to open them, but at the same time, she found it harder and harder to hold herself restrained—immobile in the bed. Her legs felt not quite painful, but not comfortable. She stopped herself from rolling side to side, not wanting to disturb Gerald.

The little house slept.

Gerald lay quietly snuffling, as he often did. Her mind drifted back to the fish tanks downstairs with their strangely sinister occupants hanging and darting in the dark. To her surprise, this too accentuated her new self-awareness. She wondered how much time had passed since Gerald came to bed. Despite the fans and the sea breeze, the house felt close, bordering on stuffy. Her nightgown clung to her skin when she moved. She peered at her watch but could not read the dial.

At length, she sat up, listening to the darkness. A light snore drifted in from Cindy's bedroom—Robert, most likely. She imagined the softness of Cindy and her child both sleeping. She revisited the desire to know Cindy better. Silently she lifted her legs, swung them over the edge of the bed, placed her bare feet lightly on the floor, and stood. Her nightgown glowed in the just-perceptible light.

She considered looking for her slippers but decided against it. After a moment of orientation, she padded quietly into the living room. Light from streetlamps outlined furniture and windows. The wooden house cracked, relaxing in the cooling night air. At the door, Lillian paused, feeling the latch with sighted fingers, then worked it open with only the faintest of clicks and stepped safely outside, squeezing the door silently shut behind her.

From her right came the repeated slap and sigh of water meeting sand and withdrawing. A soft, damp breeze pressed the gown against her skin and molded it between her legs.

At the bottom of the stairs, she ducked through the door Robert had used earlier. Streetlight seeping through the bamboo shades illuminated the tanks dimly, without revealing the fish. Nightgown flowing, Lillian stepped boldly into the room beneath the house, feeling the cool, packed sand under her bare feet. In the half-light, fish tanks surrounded her as before—their columns seeming taller now, stacked higher than she remembered. Her ears were cluttered with half-sounds.

Four long strides brought her to within inches of a column of glass. Up close, the smell of the fish was strong and sweet. Pumped air popped and gurgled. Resting her forehead against the glass, Lillian threaded her gaze through to the other side of the translucent box of water. Shapes drifted across her line of sight.

Her eyes no longer seemed actively to see, but simply to remain open, like doors left open to the night air so that half-visible shapes and images could come and go without disharmony. There was just the suggestion of the relief she used to feel with the first drink. At last she feels temporarily safe from the visual and auditory distortions that have plagued her from the beginning of this journey.

Breathing deeply, she opened herself to the eyes of a curious fish hanging before her and felt him swim into her eyes and she into his. The creatures made microscopic bumps against the glass wall. She soothed her cheek against the cool glass, feeling the tiny echoes of their contacts. Pressing breasts, belly, and thighs against the tanks before her, she fancied the faint impacts all up and down her body and responded with tingles.

The end of life lay beckoning in the tanks. Inhaling luxuriously, she embraced that massive fear. Her shoulders softened. Tightness, which usually clenched her upper belly, now warmed, releasing the muscles.

But an unwelcome violet glow suddenly exposed the tanks—far too much light. She reproached herself for relaxing so easily. But at that same moment, she still found herself thinking, *Yes, it's easy, the slipping away of the hope that anyone might have held me safe.* She has seen it and survived.

And it was e-a-s-y, like learning in a dream that she can breathe underwater when she has been just at the point of drowning. A resonant voice she recognized as her own told her, *Just breathe, Lil. Just breathe, and I will hold you.*

She breathed lazily in the cool easiness of it.

"Mother?"

Lillian's face hides from the searching word.

"Mother, what is it?" Cindy cried.

The light was on—the florescent bulb Robert installed this afternoon. Lillian stood back from the tanks. Peaceful sadness washed over her, and she began to cry like warm rain.

"Oh, Mother," Cindy said, at once repelled and compelled to help in spite of her inclinations, putting her arms around Lillian—the young mother instinctively giving comfort. Lillian stood passively, arms at her sides, soaking it in. Finally, Cindy drew away.

Lillian stood up straight and willed the tears to stop.

Cindy peered into her face. "Are you all right? Oh, look at the dirt on your little face." She wiped her mother's face with her hand as she would an unknown child's. "And your gown's all dirty, all down the front."

Lillian was not certain that she still possessed the gift of speech. "I'm . . ." she croaked.

"Mother, what were you doing here?" Cindy asked, a little harshly now that her initial fear has passed. "I heard the door, and I checked your bed and you were gone—just Daddy sleeping, and I didn't want to wake him. And then I came down here, and there you were, standing there, pressed all up against the aquariums. It's so creepy in here, and there you were in the middle of it all. Oh, Mother, you're not drinking again, are you? Do you like my baby? Do you know I imagine sometimes with her that I am you? Isn't that silly?"

"Thank . . . y . . . ," Lillian began, voice breaking again. She cleared her throat. "Thank you, dear, for coming down for me." With an effort, she focused on her daughter. "You're anything but silly, and your baby is beautiful, and I'm not drinking."

Feeling that she should say more, she could think of nothing else to say. Finally, she broke the silence. "I think I'll go back to bed now." She smiled as best she could but knew somehow that she must have been frightening to contemplate. Cindy was staring at her dirty feet.

Lillian looked down at the feet, undeniably hers and inexplicably filthy. Unable to suppress a chuckle, she said gently and with what felt like great warmth for her only child, "They're feet, dear."

Wide-eyed, Cindy sucked in her breath as she stepped back.

Lillian looked at her curiously. "I'm sorry, dear. I didn't say that to hurt you." After a pause, she continued. "Please don't be frightened of me, Cindy," she said reasonably, "All I needed was to see the fish one more time."

Upstairs, Lillian crossed the living room on the same nonchalant bare feet, like an ancient woman approaching a well (*All I need is an earthen jug*, she thought, suppressing a smile.) She entered the bedroom, pulled the soiled satin nightgown over her head, dropped it to the floor, and slipped into the bed beside her sleeping husband. She lay naked on her back, feeling the sweet breeze from the windows and fans play over her softening body. Delaying pulling up the sheet, she paused to enjoy the limpness of the muscles in her shoulders and belly. She sighed. She could not recall ever having felt this way. Fearless, she sank into sleep.

When Lillian woke the next morning, her heart was pounding. The light was bright behind the venetian blinds, and she was damp with sweat. Gerald was not in the bed, and no sound came from the house. She first remembered the fish and then realized that she was naked. She remembered falling asleep naked. Gerald must have pulled the sheet over her in the night, thank God. The scent of coffee and toast lingered in the heavy air, but no sounds drifted in from the kitchen.

Climbing out of bed, she picked up her nightgown from where it lay on the floor. She winced when she looked at the stains down the front, streaks no doubt from the dusty aquariums. She folded the gown so that the stains did not show and slipped it under the pillow. Hurriedly, she collected panties and brassiere from beside the suitcase, quickly covering her nakedness with them. She stepped into yesterday's rumpled blue seersucker skirt, slipped on a white blouse, buttoned it quickly, tucked it in, and finished fastening the skirt.

Opening the bag, she found her brush and brushed back her hair. She made up the bed carefully, conscious of the soiled gown under the pillow. Then, curious at the silence, she walked barefoot out into the living room. Empty. Continuing into the small kitchen, she found cups and plates stacked beside the sink, ready for washing. The coffeepot was empty.

She filled the kettle and turned on the gas fire under it. Efficiently, she cleaned the coffee grounds out of the basket of the pot and rinsed the basket clean. She rinsed out the pot. In the third cabinet she opened, she found ground coffee, which she measured into the aluminum basket. From the small window over the sink, she could see the bay and a spit of sand, littered with chairs, a bicycle, toys, a beached skiff, and the skeletal ruin of a larger boat. Beside the bicycle, two children leaned together, apparently in earnest conversation.

When the kettle beside her began its first tentative sounds before whistling, she lifted the pot to block the whistle, turned off the fire, and poured hot water into the reservoir on top of the coffeepot, listening with pleasure to the sound the fresh coffee made as it dripped and splashed into the empty aluminum container. The odor of the dripping coffee wreathed her. She closed her eyes, gratefully inhaling the quotidian smell, willing her heart to slow down. Despite a suffocating sense of foreboding, she was hungry. She smiled self-indulgently at this discovery.

As she turned back to the window, the two children she had noticed before—heads still bent toward each other—walked out of her line of vision. The part of the beach she could see remained empty. From across the bay came the incessant chugging of whatever machine was at work over there. She remembered the sound from last night and wondered if it had been there, unnoticed, the whole time. When the coffee had finished dripping, she rinsed out one of the stacked cups, filled it with coffee, and padded across the living room.

As it had the night before, the door opened quietly, this time admitting morning light and heat. The light fish-salty smell of the Gulf of Mexico rode on the soft air. Lillian made her way halfway down the long stairs and sat comfortably, allowing a new trembling in her hands to subside,. She took another deep breath and then another, settling herself resolutely. Inhaling the coffee smell, she pursed her lips and skimmed off a cautious first sip, just the coolest top layer of hot liquid. Once more, she breathed deeply.

"I don't know. I don't know." Cindy's voice came up to her from under the house.

A mumble from Gerald, followed by silence. More unintelligible speech, then Gerald said clearly, "I thought I smelled it on her after we left the café we stopped at in Shreveport, but I don't see where she could have gotten it. I didn't smell anything last night."

Finally, Robert's more resonant voice carried clearly. "Well, look, I don't want to butt into this. You know that. Don't want to be in the decision making. But I'll be glad to drive up to school and call around. Probably find somebody in Gainesville to see her. Maybe the hospital up there. I doubt she needs a sanitarium or anything like that. Maybe just a hospital room for a day or two to get herself oriented while she's being monitored."

Lillian felt herself as still and alert as a deer in a meadow.

"It's just so sad!" Cindy said. "She's always been a little . . . strange, you know? But up there against the glass, moving like . . ."

"Gerald's soothing voice murmurs, "It's okay, sweetheart."

Cindy's voice interrupted itself, broken by crying. "She was *disgusting*! I'm sorry, but that's what she was!"

Now Lillian could hear Cindy settle into a rhythm of sobbing and catching her breath. Gerald continued to murmur. Suddenly, the baby cried out, and Cindy cried, in response, "Oh nooo! I'm sorry, Lovie. Mommy's sorry, sweetie. Mommy's so sorry."

Under cover of the baby's cries and Cindy's comforting murmurs, Lillian tiptoed up the stairs and quietly let herself back into the house.

In the kitchen again, she stared out the window, trying to decide what to do. Her shoes were still under the sink from last night. She noticed her purse on the coffee table with the car keys beside it. Pushing her feet into the loafers, she picked up the keys and the purse as the others came back into the house, the baby still crying. As they trooped into the kitchen, she turned to face them and—without thinking—backed against the wall and braced her arm on the countertop, the keys dangling from her fingers. She straightened her posture and waited, the purse tucked under her free arm.

At last, little Emily stopped crying.

"Well!" Lillian slipped briskly into the ensuing silence. "If we have time, I was just leaving. I need to pick up some things at the drugstore I saw on the corner, and after that, I could use a shower. Gerald," she said and almost laughed when he jumped, his eyes staring at her, "the car was almost out of gas last night. Give me the gasoline card and I'll get it filled up." The others remained in mute tableau, which she was dismayed to see zoom away to the small end of the telescope.

Later, she would say ruefully, "I couldn't help thinking, 'All they lacked was some sheep and a cow or two. Three kings. Couple of shepherds.'"

"I made some more coffee," she offered because they seemed to have been standing silently a long time. It was as though they weren't able to hear her. She half expected that when they finally spoke, captions would crawl across the bottom of the screen as in a foreign movie.

"I knew I had to get out then, and that I didn't have much time before they came to life and started moving again," she explained later when it was all over. "It was like I already knew every move I was going to make just before I made it."

Lillian took a step toward the hall door. Gerald was standing in her way, almost as though he intended to obstruct her passing, but diffident as ever. "Gerald?" she prompted, smiling warmly and holding out her hand, palm up.

He looked at her blankly.

"The card?"

"Oh," he said. Automatically, he removed his wallet from his hip pocket, extracted the gasoline credit card, and handed it to her.

"Thank you," she said. "I won't be long. Just some women things."

Gerald remained where he was, apparently lost in thought.

"Excuse me," Lillian said. At last, he moved aside, allowing her to pass him. She straightened her back as she went, deciding that a shower would take too long. Her straight back felt comfortable and relaxed.

Over her shoulder, she threw a smile to Cindy and said, "I'll wash off my feet, dear, when I get back."

Crashing and Burning

Jonah's stupor begins, then, as an escape from the common human fear; he alone sleeps instead of crying out, as God and common sense require him to do. His flight takes on an aspect of withdrawal from himself, from his own voice, his own depths. If his flight is downward, into the depths of the ship, the depths of the sea, these fail to achieve metaphorical resonance. Jonah plumbs literal depths without touching any chord of mystery in his soul.[5]

—Avivah Gottlieb Zornberg, *The Murmuring Deep*

My tongue wakes me up, playing in fissures in my lips. Heat on the side of my face—from the window no doubt. I'm hot and sick at my stomach, exhausted from chasing sleep. People die in closed cars in this kind of sun. Afternoon? Eyes throbbing behind the lids. A pulse in my throat. Why am I trembling?

Waking up again. My muscles don't belong to me. Is that dehydration? Suffocation? The window crank is hot. With this heat, it's got to be afternoon—but what day? I tried opening the window, but it didn't help much. My blouse is drenched, chilly on my belly. The plastic car seat is wet against my back. Sweat or tears? Time? Is that me groaning? Pieces of days stretching back. My heart is trying to break though my chest. The pulse over my eyes and in my throat is in time with the pounding. Get out. Get out now.

I definitely heard myself groaning as I opened the door, then the retching sound. The vomit burned my throat. My head was hanging well out, away from the car. Not much came up. I fell back against the hot car seat, breathless and exhausted, the strong, sour taste of vomit in my nose and

---

[5.] Avivah Gottlieb Zornberg, *The Murmuring Deep* (New York: Schoken Books, 2009), 83.

mouth. I remember thinking, *Well, I guess I can still vomit.* When I smiled at my own drollery, the cracks in my lips hurt. It served me right. I was afraid to open my eyes.

I remembered having seen a rusty iron water faucet at the front edge of the parking lot on the beach. After a while, when I had pretty well caught my breath, I opened my eyes and then pushed open the door again and struggled to get out. Another wave of nausea caught me when I moved. I carefully put my left foot on the ground, avoiding the vomit on the sparse grass and sand. Then the right foot. My sweaty thighs stuck to the seat. Both bare feet were on the dry, prickly grass. A pair of new-looking flip-flops of black, red, and green leather were on the floor in front of the driver's seat. I tossed them out onto the ground and pushed my feet into them. I pulled myself upright, and having experienced a powerful tiredness in my lower back, I twisted around to lean on the car top, content to allow it to burn the inside of my arm.

Two little girls were playing on a jungle gym. They stopped and gazed at me with the solemnity kids are famous for. The older girl looked to be six or so. She casually fell back and hung from her knees from a top bar. The little one I guessed was prekindergarten. I smiled at them, pushed myself up off the car, and took one step, trying not to sway. Steadying, I picked my way to the water faucet, watching for broken glass and stickers. I started to bend straight over the faucet from my hips but then remembered the kids and turned sideways to them, squatted, and tucked my skirt tail up under me.

For a scary second, I thought I couldn't feel panties under the skirt, but there they were, soggy and binding. *My lord,* I thought, *I must be a sight to behold!*

Rusty water ran hot out of the faucet. I liked the way it felt running over my hand. As I waited for it to clear, I looked over at the girls and said, "Hi." The older girl nudged the younger one, who looked at her and made a face before returning her gaze to me; and both of them said, "Hi," in unison. I fell in love with their voices.

Evidently, they had taken my speaking to them as an invitation because when I looked again, they had climbed down from the jungle gym and were coming my way. They drew up in front of me, and the older girl asked, "Are you going to have a baby?"

"I don't *think* so," I said with some surprise. "Why do you ask?"

The little one piped up, "'Cause . . . 'fore our baby brother was bornded, our mommy trowed up ever day." She looked up to the older girl, who nodded her confirmation. She twisted her torso and twirled her skirt

"So you have a baby brother now?" I offered, just to hear them speak again, though all I got this time were more nods. "What are your names, if I may ask?"

"I'm Julie," the older girl said, "and this is Sissie. What's yours?"

"I'm Lillian," I said automatically, wondering if I should have said "Mrs. Stallings" or "Ms. Lillian."

I glanced down at my hand, still under the faucet, and had the weirdest feeling that I hadn't seen it in some time. The water had filled my cupped palm and was running over onto the ground. I watched the movement of the water and the distortion it brought to my engagement and wedding rings. Gently, I dipped my face into the flow and took a sip. It was surprisingly sweet on my tongue. The thought came that if necessary, I could pawn my rings, but just acknowledging it made me almost nauseous with guilt.

A chill ran down my back, incongruous in the heat, and a feverishness tingled at my hair roots. I was thirsty but afraid of being sick again if I swallowed more. I tried another sip then rinsed out my mouth. My throat felt almost ready to tolerate swallowing.

Julie's hair was up in a French braid. I told her I liked it and asked who had done it for her. She seemed to be in deep thought about something else and didn't answer. "Did your mommy do it?" I asked after a while.

"Where did your friends go?" she asked me at length. Taken by surprise, I guessed it was my turn to ponder. I didn't want to admit to not knowing who she was talking about. Finally, I said, "Uhh . . . maybe they had to go to work."

"Your husband too?"

A thrill of fear caught in my chest and belly. "My husband? Did somebody say he was my husband?"

"No." Both girls were laughing.

"Then what makes you think he was my husband?"

Little Sissie jumped up and down, shrieking and giggling. "Cause you was kissin'! Out in the water!"

I felt my face grow hot, and a giant space opened in my stomach. Mercifully, a woman who had appeared across the road from the beach was calling the girls. Julie said formally, "That's our mommy. We have to go now, but maybe we will come back and talk to you some more this afternoon."

"Well, thank you. I would like that," I said, matching her serious tone. Then I waved at their mother and watched anxiously, checking in both directions for cars, as she shepherded the two of them across the road.

From my squatting position, I bent my head for another sip of the sweet water. To my right, the continuing low sound of the surf reasserted itself. Through my hanging hair, I looked across the expanse of bright white beach. It reminded me of angel food cake lying strangely near the translucent turquoise water. I graphically imagined the water melting the cake.

The beach was familiar, all the more tantalizing after my talk with the children. Partial memories of people and fragments of voices swirled around in me as I squatted there.

My feet were sandy, top and bottom and between my toes, and there was sand all over the floor of the car. Also, I couldn't remember buying the new flip-flops. A man's voice echoed in my mind, saying, *We gotta get you some beach shoes.*

A name just out of reach. My hair smells of wood smoke, another story to wonder about. Maybe a long one. Then I remembered that I had worn loafers on the trip to Florida and when I fled Cindy's house, and I couldn't remember having seen them in the car. "So I may need to buy shoes if I ever get back to where people wear them."

In bare feet the night before I fled, I had crept down the outside stairs in the dark while the house was sleeping and let myself into Robert's work room with the fish tanks. Once again, I had flowed through the eyes of the fish hanging stealthily in the dark aquariums. Now I long to feel it again.

I walked back to the car. The keys were in the ignition. Used paper cups and plates, empty soda bottles, clothing, and plastic utensils littered the backseat and floor. A gust of fear blew through me as I realized that my purse didn't seem to be in the car. I yanked the keys out of the ignition and hurried to open the trunk After a moment of searching, I spotted the purse in a cardboard box. "Thank god!"

I realized that I had been holding my breath, and now I let it out. My wallet was in the purse, along with my checkbook; and in the wallet, I found the gasoline credit card and $37 in cash. There was also a pint Popov vodka bottle in the box with a little less than an inch of vodka left at the bottom. I closed the trunk and, returning to the front of the car, put my purse and the bottle on the front seat and got back in. I started the car and drove to a small grocery store down the street and bought an orange Crush and a local newspaper. The fuel gauge showed a quarter full.

As I was pulling back into the deserted parking lot later, something I registered down at the end of drive froze my blood. I parked the car again and walked to the end of the lot. Below a low wall, a water pipe projected up from a concrete floor that had a drain in the center. Halfway up the pipe was a shower handle, and at the top, I saw three showerheads. At about knee level, a regular outside water faucet—like the one I had been using out on the beach—projected out from the pipe. A partial memory of washing off sand and salt here late at night, without a bathing suit.

Back in the car, with the air conditioner running, I sorted through the paper trash on the floor and used my skirt to wipe out one of the cleaner cups, filled it part way with vodka, and then filled it up the rest the way with orange Crush. I took a mouthful and held it to get accustomed to the taste, then tried to swallow. After two more attempts, I was able to keep down the mouthful. I sat for a while, feeling the deep warming as the vodka moved down through my esophagus and into my stomach.

After a while, I drank down the rest of the cupful. Again, I waited, feeling the familiar appearance of sweat on my face. If I was sweating, I wasn't too dehydrated. Gradually, my hands stopped trembling, and I felt myself relax one bundle of muscles at a time. I unfolded the newspaper and looked at the date—Wednesday, August 1, 1960. The clock on the dashboard said ten fifteen. With a foolish sense of relief and even inexplicable satisfaction, I was pleased to have gotten so much done so early in the day.

The town had grown stale and barren in the midmorning glare. Suddenly reminded of the possibility of being found by Gerald and the imaginary posse, I started the car again and drove it out of the parking lot, past the shower, and down the street until I saw a sign that said Highway 90. I still didn't know where I was, although the sun was behind me, so I guessed that I was heading west.

The vodka had pretty well taken away my headache and some of the guilt and fear. More importantly, I was finally feeling some hunger and thirst. Returning to the little park, I got out and moved gingerly back to what I had come to think of as *my* water faucet and drank as much as I could.

I moved the car closer to a trash barrel and climbed into the backseat, pulled a plastic bag out of the pile of trash, and began sorting through the debris, stopping every few moments to rest and sigh while the trembling in my hands settled down; and I tracked the rivulets of sweat down my neck and sides and down the sides of my the brazier. Soda cans and bottles were mixed with paper plates, empty vodka bottles, wet bathing suits and underwear—men's and women's—and a wet pair of men's jeans. I had not brought clothes with me when I fled, so I prayed that one of the suits was one I had bought.

Then in a new rush of anxiety, I set aside one of the bathing suits that looked like it would fit and threw the others into the plastic bag. The one I had chosen was free of sand and did not feel salty. An empty Southern Comfort bottle surprised me because I hate the taste of Southern Comfort. I couldn't remember drinking from the bottle. Chicken bones and trash lay in a box from a fried chicken take-out that I vaguely remembered.

While scooping up a pile of paper trash to put in the bag, my hand fell on something cold and limp with a milky goo inside. I felt myself recoil and thought, *So that's what "recoil" means.* Then I forced myself to use some of the paper to pick up the thing up and stick it and the paper I held it with straight into the plastic bag. I recognized that I was close to retching again but swallowed it back and rested on my heels.

My ears burned; it seemed as though they had been burning all morning, and I felt what I guessed was like the way a lack of oxygen would feel. I wondered if I had sunburned.

Finally standing up, I decided that the backseat of the car was at least free of trash, although there were some stains on the seat cover and sand on the floor. All that remained was a small zipper bag I remembered having bought in a truck stop in Fort Walton Beach the first day. I walked back to the beach faucet and splashed more water in my face.

I didn't feel at all crazy but seriously wondered how some of the bathing suits remained wet while I am dry—skirt, blouse, and all. Obviously, I had changed into and out of the bathing suit, but I didn't feel salty—sweaty, yes, but not Gulf-water salty. I looked out at the water again, willing myself to recall when I was in it. All I could think of was the outdoor shower or a motel room, which I couldn't have afforded. Suddenly, the Gulf flew into the farthest extension of my vision. I squeezed my eyes shut tight and opened them again, and the distortion had corrected itself.

I assumed that after this many days, Gerald must already have contacted the police. The thought made my heart begin pounding again, and I swallowed back more bile, but I was getting accustomed to it. The road map I had bought on the first day, now sitting on the shelf behind the backseat, was further evidence of how clear and purposeful I had been that first day compared with the sorry mess I was in now! That soon, I had already decided that Gerald would expect me to head straight for Houston. As best I had been able to figure it out, that would have been on Highway 90. But if that was four days ago, I had no idea where he would be looking now or if he was still looking or even still at Cindy's. He had closed his office for two weeks, although he still had a secretary working there who would contact him if need be.

Thinking of the first day of my escape (as I was now styling it), I remembered what it was like to reach the Alabama border, or close to it. Heart in throat, I had pulled off on a bluff overlooking the Gulf of Mexico and quickly scanned the highway in both directions as though I expected Gerald and some posse or something to come charging after me on horseback or pickup trucks. That had warranted a smile at my own expense.

I can still remember my gasp of excitement that day and the feeling so strong, it drowned out the fear that was driving me. Looking down at the beautiful greenish blue water and the low, slow waves fifty feet below, I felt the kind of uncomplicated joy I had always imagined only a child could feel. I had slept through that sight when we were passing through from Texas. Now reliving the thrill when I finally saw it, I once again found myself grinning "like a Chessie cat," momentarily not caring who saw me and hoping fervently that Cindy also had experienced feelings like that during her life so far. As on that first day, I again found myself thinking defiantly, *Come on and do your worst, buddy boy, you're not putting me in any damned loony bin!* But bringing Cindy back into my reverie was sobering.

It seemed to me that I had turned north for Hattiesburg that day before apparently returning to the coast, but I couldn't remember arriving or why I went back to the coast or with whom.

Now anxious to get myself oriented and on my way, I pulled the car around to the side of a motel parking lot in the downtown area—not for a room, but just to get the car off the street while I organized myself. I must admit though that once I had parked, a half-formed image came to me of booking a room then slipping away in the morning without paying, just to conserve my meager funds. Whatever I did, sooner or later, I was going to have to go to ground and confront the money situation and my growing exhaustion. I reached behind me for the zipper bag on the backseat.

When I walked into the lobby, the desk clerk appraised me with a slight smirk. Apparently, women still didn't travel alone very much in Mississippi. I gave him what I hoped was my most withering, level, no-nonsense gaze and asked how much he charged for a room. At the same time, I was busy adjusting my posture to make the bag look less empty. In the middle of that, I pictured myself standing there in flip-flops and a soiled and wrinkled skirt and blouse that I had been wearing (at least part of the time) for nearly a week with not even a trace of makeup. At that point, I also realized that I still had not checked my hair before getting out of the car. Nevertheless, there I stood, sweating profusely again; and for the first time, I became aware of my own body odor.

The price for one night turned out to be barely below my total resources. Briefly, I imagined running a hot bath, stripping off my soiled and sweaty clothes and washing them out, and then taking a long soak in the tub before pulling a Bonnie-and-Clyde act. Now I noticed that the desk clerk was talking to a young boy I hadn't seen before. The boy nodded and looked toward me. So much for Bonnie and Clyde. I stepped away from the desk to pretend looking through the racks of flyers advertising tourist attractions. When I looked again, the boy had disappeared.

Imagining sirens racing toward me, I strode directly out the door and around to my car, stepped in, and pulled the door closed stealthily as though that would keep anybody from noticing I had left. Without looking back, I started the motor and eased out of the parking lot.

A street sign indicated that I was on "Beach Road." Now all sorts of things were beginning to seem familiar. I decided to risk driving straight west, counting on surprise to cover me, and also hoping that Gerald and company had already searched this area while I was cavorting around, doing whatever I was doing when I should have been getting myself out of Dodge.

Leaving the town, I saw road signs indicating that I had been in Pass Christian and that I was heading for Bay St. Louis. I decided to try to get as far west as I could before nightfall. Although I had lived all my life in East

Texas and Louisiana, my stereotypes of Mississippi and Alabama were that they were semilawless, dark places where it was dangerous to be a female or in any kind of minority or alone, especially in rural areas and at night.

On the trip over, Gerald and I had listened on the car radio to news of civil rights boycotts and protests in New Orleans, and it seemed as though threats of public disorder had grown more common throughout the region. In a way, I was pleased that people were standing up for things I believed in; but now that I was alone in a place where I was vulnerable and surrounded by people who I assumed did not share my values, I was also afraid that by some magic trick, someone might read my mind and punish me for all the beliefs I had always hidden.

With all the eccentrics and misfits dangling from my ancestral line—Grandmother Louise's suicide, Uncle Gressett's strange relationship with his mother, my daddy the womanizing drunk. And *his* father, for god's sake, crazy old Mr. Joshua, on the lam fifteen years and for no reason—it's hardly amazing I didn't feel bulletproof as far as commitment to mental institutions was concerned. None of my ancestors, many of whom roundly deserved it, had ever wound up in the slammer. Nevertheless, here I was: at the first serpent's hiss of danger, terrified of being committed to a loony bin.

I hated that kind of timidity in myself. The afternoon Gerald and I arrived, I asked Cindy for the use of her shower. No sooner had I gotten myself soaped up than Cindy walked into the bathroom and announced, "Mother, I'm sorry to bother you, but I have to rinse out a diaper." I froze, unable to decide—of all things—which term of endearment to use with her while she sounded so nonchalant and businesslike.

I stood there, no doubt gawping, now unable to decide even what name to use. Not "Cindy," certainly not "Lucinda." I wanted something more comfortable and welcoming, maybe "dear" or "sweetheart." But we don't call each other things like that. Besides, I was beginning to think Cindy considered me a lunatic or an invalid or just a generic danger. But that shouldn't have kept me from calling my own child "sweetheart," should it? How strange that today I had felt so at ease with little Julie and Sissie on the beach but to not my own late adolescent kid.

Of course, in Cindy's shower—as always—I had just avoided the problem by blurting "Come on in," as cordially as I could while crouching—wet and naked as a drowned rat—behind the shower curtain.

"Sorry," Cindy said again, and I felt guilty that my daughter felt as uncomfortable around me as I did with her. I could hear the swishing of the soiled diaper in the toilet. The odor of baby poop reached my wet nose, and it was almost dear to me because it came from Cindy's daughter. Then Cindy said, "Sorry about the smell," and sort of laughed. I remember thinking, *Well, at least we can find some sort of soft intimacy in shared shit.* But then I nearly choked, swallowing my giggle.

"Mother?" Cindy said solicitously when I snorted like a horse in spite of myself. "Are you all right?" It would have been so easy—so natural—just to burst out laughing at my poor, old hung-up self, and we could have had a great mother-daughter laugh together. But I couldn't do it. My daddy would have called me a tight ass, and you know what? He would have been right. But knowing that doesn't make it any easier either to change or to put up with it.

In the shower, I could hear fresh alarm enter Cindy's voice and tried to fix it by saying, "It's all right, Cindy. I just thought of something funny." But then, in spite of myself, I continued to giggle, and realizing just how crazy that giggling probably sounded made me laugh even harder.

"Oh my," Cindy said, sounding really distraught now. I finally recovered, but it was too late, and I wound up listening helplessly—or so it seemed at the time, though of course, I have thought of a dozen things since then that I could have said or done instead of standing there—as I once heard a girl say in high school, "Like Old Kalija, the wooden Indian."

Divining from the carefully unobtrusive sounds made by the lid closing on the diaper pail and the toilet flushing just how much ground I probably had lost in the eyes of my child. And then to cap it all off, Cindy said "Oh!" again, this time as though suppressing a sob. Surprised, I listened to my dear child rushing out of the bathroom. The door slammed behind her, leaving me alone; realizing finally that in my anxiety, I had returned to laughing like a loon while the water from the shower sluiced over me, growing cooler and cooler as I drained the little family's meager hot water tank.

Of course, I couldn't help thinking of my mother and our lifelong failure to connect, and of my own anger as I watched myself becoming what I have always hated. While imagining what my mother must have felt all these years, I cringed at picturing how Cindy must see me, always withholding and now apparently losing my mind.

Back in mid-flight, the memories plunged me back into the interlude with Robert's fish the one night I had managed to spend with them. And now, just at that mental point as I was crossing the long bridge to Bay St. Louis, thinking of all my missteps with Cindy, I looked down at the sparkling bay. As I did, the memory I had been grappling with all day flooded my mind. I had actually *been in* the water! I suddenly remembered clearly, crossing over the verge into the clear water, out past where the little waves were breaking. I had looked down through the green water and could see my feet sharply defined below me, just a little distorted, but definitely my own feet and legs. The water was warm as soup. I had kept pushing out deeper, watching my legs move now, sort of hopping up each time a wave approached, then dropping down again to the sandy bottom; and then taking another micro-step out, just a little deeper.

I recalled clearly that the water by then was splashing up to my chin, and then my whole body melted and let go. It was like I could almost feel the warm water flowing through me. When I came down from the last hop, my feet just settled onto the sand and didn't hop again. My eyes were open underwater and I looked up and could see the bright surface above me. It had almost been as though I could breathe the water, but not quite. I imagined Robert's fish swimming in through my dilated pupils. Then I remembered flexing my two feet and popping up through the boundary of the surface and taking an easy breath and settling back down to the sand before the next wave arrived, bending my knees so that I could go deeper without losing contact with the bottom.

I remembered it as even more magical than the first time in Robert's work room, the interpenetration of myself and the fish had expanded to an interpermeation of all life-forms. Almost breathless with excitement and relief and a jumble of thoughts and emotions, I slowed the car and pulled over to the shoulder of the road and continued driving slowly. I was so full of emotions that I could imagine myself literally blowing up into something enormous and then exploding. I was sure that I had not been alone when I was here before, but I could not remember any details of who I was with.

Now once off the bridge and heading for Bay St. Louis, I carefully slowed my breathing. I pulled in at the first filling station I came to and filled the tank with gasoline while continuing to calm myself down. Then I went inside and pulled the phone book from under the pay telephone and leafed through to the yellow pages. I had done this once for my dad. Even though it turned out to have been too late for him, at least I had learned how.

I found the number and dialed it. After quite a few rings, a woman answered, and I asked if there was an AA meeting in town today. She said that there was one at five o'clock at the First Baptist Church on Main Street. My agitation was such that I forgot to ask the address or where to find Main Street, but it wasn't hard to find. The first large square brick building I came to was unmistakably a First Baptist Church, across the street from a hamburger place. I had a half hour to spare and realized that I was starving.

"Don't make yourself sick now," I admonished myself in my mother's voice as I pushed through the door. I ordered a plain hamburger and chocolate malt. The kid behind the counter looked at me curiously but didn't run away or slip out to call the authorities. Still, I kept my eye on him anyway—just in case—while I used the mirror behind the counter to pull my hair into place as best I could with my fingers.

Putting the tray on the little table, I sat down and closed my eyes and took several deep breaths. One of my dad's stories came to me about a time when he was waiting tables after school in a café in Monroe. Daddy said he looked up one afternoon and saw a man he knew, a widower who lived with his two grown sons on a farm outside of town a way.

He said that it was early spring, and they had just sold the first produce from their vegetable garden after a particularly hard, long winter; and they came in, walking "in a straight line like a row of ducks," headed directly to three empty stools at the counter, and sat down without saying a word or changing expression.

Daddy said that the father, who was holding the money they had been paid for their produce and was clearly in charge, was salivating so copiously that he had to suck up the surplus saliva before each word he spoke. Daddy imitated him blurting out, "*Slurp. Slurp.* Three bowls of chili!" That line never failed to draw a laugh when we repeated it to each other.

With that comforting expression in my ears, I carefully chewed each bite of the hamburger—continuing to compose myself, regulating my breathing and allowing all my body parts to absorb the nutrients. So then I went next door to the graceless old red brick building, and it finally came my time to talk. I listened to everybody introducing themselves, and when it came my turn, I just spoke right up like I had been doing it all my life and said,

"Hello, everybody, my name is Lillian Stallings. I'm visiting from Texas, and I don't know whether I'm an alcoholic or not. I really don't think so, but my daddy sure was one, and I been to a few of these meetings with him." That brought a friendly scattering of chuckles and bought me enough time to think for a moment, and finally to say, "I think I came here this afternoon just to get a little peace and friendship before I head on out to where I have to get to tonight." That seemed to cover it pretty well, so I sat back down and smiled back at the applause and nodded my thanks and garnered the delicate sliver of contentment that blew through my body.

Part Two
The Making of an Alligator Wrestler

>   Normally we come into the world headfirst, like divers into the pool of humanity. Besides, the head has a soft spot through which the infant soul, according to the traditions of the body symbolism, could still be influenced by its origins. The slow closing of the head's fontanel and fissures, its hardening into a tightly sealed skull, signified separation from an invisible beyond and final arrival here. Descent takes a while. We grow down, and we need a long life to get on our feet.[6]

>   James Hillman. The Soul's Code

[6.] James Hillman. The Soul's Coide: In search of character and calling., (New York: Random House) 1996, 42

A Counterfeit Cajun

> *The adults are not fully competent with their own instruments, but there is nobody else for the child to appeal to. Children go on asking, of course, but eventually they have to settle for the adults' exhausted impatience, and the fictions of life.*[7]
>
> —Adam Phillips, *Terrors and Experts*

One thing Lou Fontenot liked to say about his time in the Great War was that when they signed the armistice, he definitely was not ready to go home. He said that partly because he doubted that most people expected him to say it, but also because it was true. After arriving in France in June of 1918, he contracted the "Spanish" flu almost immediately and recovered just in time to join his unit for the bloody "Hundred Days Offensive" still feeling a little "puny," as his mother would have said.

Sometimes he would even add that France was about the only place he had ever felt like he belonged. At times, he still thinks that was true too; but at other times, he is not so sure. When he says he never belonged anywhere before, he mostly has in mind where he grew up. He was a native of Lafayette Parish in southwestern Louisiana, home to hundreds of "Cajuns" who speak a French dialect and trace their ancestry to French-speaking colonists expelled by the British from northeastern Canada in the mid-eighteenth century. Eventually, they made their way to the area around Lafayette Parish, and Lou's father's people are descended from them.

Outside Lafayette Parish, Lou is quick to clarify that in truth, only his father's family were Cajuns. His mother, having been born and raised in northern Louisiana by people who spoke only English, lived in Texas

---

[7.] Adam Phillips, *Terrors and Experts* (Cambridge, Mass.: Harvard University Press, 1995), 1.

and Arkansas and generally looked down upon Cajuns—including Lou's father—as being socially, "racially," mentally, and morally inferior to the descendents of the Anglo-American colonizers.

When Lou was eleven, his father and his oldest brother, Joseph, were found dead in their drifting pirogue boat. Nobody ever knew for sure who killed them or why, but the assumption was that it had something to do with alligator poaching or other illegal activities. Of course, that tended to confirm the opinions shared by Lou's mother's family, that Cajuns in general—and Lou's father in particular—were "no damned good." Lou's mother probably expressed the local consensus when she told a friend, "If the damned fools had 'a behaved themselves, they wouldn't be dead now, and we wouldn't be so poor."

During the first year after the deaths, Lou's mother sometimes played with the younger kids—joking, teasing, and laughing. At those times, it would appear that things were getting back to normal with her. But then, the color would fade from her face, and she would fall silent again. Gradually, the periods of playfulness grew farther apart until by the time Lou was fourteen, when she hardly spoke at all.

Lou's older brother Claude, who automatically became head of the family after their father's death, had little time to waste speculating about the circumstances of the shooting. Claude, like his maternal ancestors, had always distrusted talkative people and tried to limit his own speech to situations that required some action. He worked the few acres of land that belonged to the family and sharecropped another eighty-odd acres—using Lou and their other brother, Tomás—to cultivate the crops and to help the two girls feed the chickens, pigs, cows, and a horse, as well as milking whatever cow was fresh at the time and mucking out the barn.

Tomás was two years older than Lou. He was wiry, nimble, and dark; whereas at fifteen, white-blond Lou was already sturdier and six inches taller than Tomás and was still growing. Unlike Lou, Tomás was graceful at dances and gallant with girls. Almost automatically, he had picked up the ability to play the accordion, and women of all ages loved to dance with him. He married young but seemed unfettered by his change of status.

The younger of the boys' sisters, Marie Lynn, was a year younger than Lou, and in some ways was his closest friend. Marie Lynn and her older sister, Jeanine, helped their mother with household chores and the meager livestock until Jeanine married, got pregnant, and moved out. Unfortunately, Jeanine's husband was killed in a bar fight less than a year later, so she and her baby son moved back to the family place and stayed. At seventeen, Tomás married a pretty girl named Carla and went to live with her family—who had more space and more money than his own family—leaving Lou, dour Claude, and gloomy Jeanine and her son Tomás (after his uncle) at home with Mama and Marie Lynn.

As soon as congress declared war on Germany in April of 1917, Tomás joined the marines, assuring young Carla that the war wouldn't last long, that he would be fine, and that she and the baby would be safe and well cared for by her parents until he got back. Lou privately wondered which way Tomás was running—forward or away—but he never asked. Later, Lou thought of asking the same question of himself.

The declaration of war against Germany came two months before Lou graduated from the eighth grade, which was as far as the local school went. To attend secondary school, children whose families could afford it—or who had members living in urban places—moved to one of the larger towns such as Lafayette, Lake Charles, or Baton Rouge and lived with relatives while attending high school. Nobody else in Lou's immediate family had finished eighth grade, and none lived in town.

On the last day of school, Lou walked over to the little library tucked away behind the kitchen in the schoolhouse and asked the librarian, Mrs. Martin, if he could still borrow books. She was a gaunt, gray, angular woman who had always treated Lou kindly. She glanced around to see if anyone was listening and said, "Well, I'm not supposed to, but you love to read so much, I guess we can give it a try. Probably best not to mention it though."

Lou and Mrs. Martin conspired to keep him in books for that summer. He would drop by casually when she was in the library, and he would take the book he had just finished from behind the bib of his overalls and wedge the new one she was loaning him into the same hiding place; he would leave unobtrusively a few minutes later. He had been reading novels for the past two years without bothering to notice who the authors were. Now he had to start paying attention to the authors so he could tell Mrs. Martin which books he would like to read next.

With Tomás gone, Lou made up his mind to help Claude until the crops were in that fall, but no longer. Meanwhile, he found an old cardboard suitcase back under one of the beds in the room where he and Claude slept. He fixed the handle on it and a clasp that kept it together and cleaned it up as best he could; and when the time came, he put his socks and drawers, his white shirt and good pants, his suspenders, and his Sunday shoes in the suitcase.

His mother was off somewhere with Jeanine and her son, but Marie Lynn saw him walking out the back door with the suitcase and ran to him and grabbed his arms and said, "Oh, brother, don't go." She pushed her blonde hair out of her face and squinted up at him. "There won't be a home no more if everybody leaves. Do you hear me?" She searched his face for a response and finally added, "Anyway, you aren't but a year older than me, and that's too young to just up and quit the family. We're still children, brother." She grabbed his upper arms with strong fingers. "Don't you know that?"

Lou told her he was sorry. "I would take you with me if I could, but you know I can't." He asked her to give Jeanine and Mama a kiss goodbye from him. She threw her arms around his neck, and he held her for a couple of minutes with her squeezing his neck and swallowing her tears until he could feel himself choking up. Finally, he cleared his throat and lifted her arms away from his neck and told her he loved her and to be a good girl and that she could always call on him in time of need, and then he walked off across the yard and down the road without risking a look back.

At fifteen, Lou was a big, strapping teenager with a farmer's skills and a grown farmer's hands. He could plant, chop, and pick cotton; and cultivate corn, beans, and most other garden crops. He could drive horses, mules, and oxen; milk cows; butcher hogs; throw together rude buildings; fix most things that broke on a farm or elsewhere; and cook what he needed to eat. He hired on with a carnival as a roustabout, feeding and exercising animals and shoveling out their cages, and putting up tents and breaking them down. That job only lasted a couple of weeks though. His size soon caught the attention of the owner and the carnival's aging prize fighter, whose job it was to challenge local men at towns the carnival visited to see if they could beat him in the ring. An assistant collected and held the money; and of course, some of the carnies doubled as shills, who would bet with house money to pump up the crowd.

Most importantly, Stella, the carnival's belly dancer and informal public relations agent, had spotted Lou his first day on the job and appointed herself his caretaker and promoter. She insisted that he take over the prize fighting job in the carnival so that he could make some decent money. She told Lou flat out that he wasn't as good in bed as he looked, but she bet he could be mean as hell at prize fighting. It turned out later that Stella was the sister of the reigning "Killer" Cooper, who was slowing down and wearing out and, she thought, was in danger of getting permanently injured. She told Cooper he needed to quit while he still had at least a teaspoonful of brain left in his head.

When the day came for Lou's first fight, the carnival was in Eunice, outside of Baton Rouge. Lou didn't want to be caught staring, but he couldn't keep his eyes off the big farmer who had paid money to take his chance at fighting the "Butcher Boy," as Lou was being billed. The farmer had a following of friends who laughed and catcalled, simultaneously urging their friend to "beat the tar out of that snot-nosed kid," and shouting that they were sure the kid was going to take him apart and put him back together again.

Killer Cooper was in Lou's corner of the ring, advising Lou on how to handle the fight. "Lead him on for a round or two, so they have time to get started betting," he said. "Make it look like he's going to win so they will bet against you."

Lou found that he had difficulty concentrating on what Cooper was saying. Actually (because of his size, he had always assumed), he had seldom been pushed to the point of a fistfight while growing up, and he now found himself gulping air and lacking skills. From somewhere deep in his childhood came an overwhelming desire to look pitiful, obedient, and helpful; as though if he did, either the farmer wouldn't want to hurt him or Cooper might step in to fight the man for him. He wanted to remind Cooper that he wasn't sixteen yet. But before that thought was fully formed, Cooper was pushing him to his feet and was walking with him to the center of the ring, where the referee said a few incomprehensible words as Lou breathed loudly through his nose and avoided meeting the farmer's eyes.

Lou was close enough to the man to catch a strong smell of alcohol. That frightened him further at first but then allowed just a whisper of hope. Although his father had been dangerous when he was drinking, it also made him slow witted and awkward. By the time his daddy was killed, Lou and Tomás usually could run away from him without a beating.

The bell rang, and Lou and the farmer began circling each other. Catcalls from the crowd made Lou worry that he and the farmer might be taking too long to get started actually fighting. He wished he could ask for advice. Just then, there was a crashing blow above his right eye as though—he said later—he had run full tilt into a tree. He staggered back, amazed at how hard he had been hit, wondering if he was cut and bleeding, wondering if his skull was broken and if he was going to lose consciousness or the sight of his eye—or even die.

The farmer ran after him, fists flailing, as though inspired by landing the first blow. Lou backed up, protecting his face with fists and arms. More blows landed. Another hammer shot hit the left side of his head. He was enveloped by the farmer's alcohol breath. Lou's body remembered being thrashed by his drunken father for misbehaving. His body's own physical memories recognized the pain, and the brain part of the body recalled the fear and the smell. On its own, his body began to fold in the middle for protection. More than anything, he wanted to jump over the ropes and run. Another heavy blow, and his legs became unstable. He sensed that if he was going to do something to avoid losing this fight, he'd better do it while he still had legs.

The farmer was swinging right and left, confident of a win and no longer bothering to protect himself, so Lou straightened up quickly and hit him as hard as he could in the face. Surprised, the farmer momentarily stopped punching and stared. Lou hit him again as he stood there. The farmer seemed solid, but he wobbled. Lou hit him once with each fist, fast and hard.

The man's arms dropped to his sides. Lou leaned back and swung at the head with all his might, connecting just at the left cheekbone, his right fist seeming to drive on through and beyond its target—the nearest thing to a "sweet spot" in prize fighting. The man crumpled to the ground like a steer in a packing house chute.

Lou felt like crying but didn't dare. He and Killer walked through the crowd to the dressing tent, and once inside, Lou sobbed shamelessly. "You done okay," Cooper said, rubbing his shoulders. "You could of led him on a little longer, to let the bets build, but for your first fight, you wasn't bad."

Gradually, Lou got used to the idea that he was going to be fighting several times a week. He usually won, but not always. Either way, he was getting hurt a lot. He broke the little finger on his left hand. His nose broadened and developed a permanent sideways crook, and he sometimes had trouble breathing through it. Scar tissue began to build up in noticeable ridges over his eyebrows. He soon tired of the constantly deepening dread of the next day's fight that never entirely stopped dogging him.

By March of 1918, Tomás had been in the marines almost a year. From his letters, he seemed to be having a wonderful time, though you could expect old Tomás to have a pretty good time wherever he was. Lou was sixteen by then, but with his size and the alterations eight months of prize fighting had wrought on his face, he looked several years older. At last, he persuaded Stella, his belly-dancing protector, to pretend to be his mother and swear to the army recruiter that he was eighteen.

The ruse succeeded, and by June, Lou was in Europe with the American Expeditionary Force—safe at last from the terrifying prize fights, hoping to find Tomás over there. He liked the countryside and the farm people. Though his Cajun dialect was a little hard for people to understand, he could pretty much figure out what they were saying. They treated him well, and to some of the women, he was a hero.

Soon after arriving at the front, Lou saw the first corpse out of the scores of dead men, horses, and mules he was to encounter during the war. The man was lying on his back with his arms flung out to the sides and his right leg curled at an awkward angle up under his side. Staring at the sky, he could have been resting after a picnic.

Lou couldn't see a wound. Curious, he circled the corpse, wondering if he dared touch it to turn it over—looking for a hole from a bullet or a bayonet. Then he saw the right side of the face and head, at least where they had been. The nose was intact, but just to the right of it, the forehead, cheek, and ear were gone. Lou could see the base of the tongue and a couple of bloody teeth where the cheek had been. The rest was an unrecognizable dark bloody pulp with bits of protruding bone.

Incongruously, an eyeball dangled from a chord of flesh, lying at about the spot where the ear should have been. The other eye was filmed over but placid looking. A blood-blackened brain was exposed where the right temple had been. Ants swarmed over the gore, picking their way in and out of cavities, racing off into the grass with their bloody treasures. Lou had an image of the man gradually being transported bit by bit into a giant anthill—shoes, uniform, cartridge belt, canteen, and all. The smell of rotting meat was faint. He had not been dead long.

Lou was one of the artillerymen who bogged down in the mud at Saint-Mihiel early in September, and by the end of that month, he was part of the American assault through the Argonne Forest. He drove mule teams to haul the heavy howitzers, dragged cases of shells, and dug trenches. He learned that war, like practically everything else he had tried so far, was mostly hard work—that and the reflexive fear of becoming just another one of the monstrous dead. But before long, even the fear grew stale and heavy, just another burden. Years later, somebody told Lou that some college historian was claiming it was the Spanish flu that beat the Germans because they were too sick to fight. All Lou could think to say was that he sure would have hated to meet up with them when they was feeling good.

Not only did Lou's Cajun French serve him well enough in the weeks immediately after the armistice, but also his love of wine and ability to drink a lot of it and still function added to the persona he cultivated. He met people with whom he was comfortable and who seemed to like him, and he began building a fantasy of remaining in France. So many workers had been killed, disabled, or dislocated that jobs were plentiful. Maybe, he thought, he could persuade Tomás to bring Carla and their son over; and together, they might establish their own little clan, maybe even inviting their younger sister, Marie Lynn, to join them. It was really much nicer in France than at home, and his fantasy of gathering his favorite kin around him became a source of deep contentment.

Coming back to camp early one morning, ducking into the tent and making his way to his cot, genitals warm and relaxed, tasting the residue of wine and enjoying the ghosts of perfume hovering on his skin, he discovered an envelope lying on his cot—the first letter he had ever received. He opened it curiously. It was signed by Marie Lynn. "Dear brother," it began, "We got a telegraph. Our Tomás is killed, we hope you are alive. We hope you can find how he died, and did he say anything or leave it for Carla and little Calvin. Come home soon as you can, dear brother, so we don't loos you to."

Lou sat on his cot and thought of Tomás, trying to avoid transforming him in his mind's eye into one of the familiar cadavers. He went out to the latrine and vomited up his wine. He wanted to go sit down somewhere and think his fill of Tomás, like drinking cool spring water, but they were waking up everybody for reveille. In the end, he was shipped back to the United States without learning how Tomás had died.

For several months, Lou traded on his status as returning "war hero," although he did not feel like one. He tracked down the carnival and fought a couple of times, but he no longer had the stomach or the tolerance for it. It was worse than a waste of time. He paid his respects to Stella and moved on. The following year, the Eighteenth Amendment went into effect, creating a niche for which Lou was well suited—working as a bouncer and a general handyman at a succession of speakeasies and bordellos.

He lived frugally in boarding houses and faithfully remitted a part of his earnings to Claude to help with the upkeep of their mother and sisters. As soon as he had saved a little money, he bought a used Ford Model T coupe. He spent most of his time in small towns at the margins of Cajun country, between Lafayette and the Texas-Louisiana border. Arriving in a new town, he would find a boarding house, settle in with his few possessions, and then locate the local library.

Lou would check out a book and take it back to his room, along with a small jar of "shine" or the occasional lucky bottle of wine from work, and take off his shoes and curl up in bed and read until he went to sleep. As time went on, he developed the habit of waking up in the night with a slight hangover and having a short drink to smooth it out. Waiting for the return of sleep, he would read for another half hour or maybe pause to make a few notes to help his memory.

He was asleep in his room one night a couple of years after the war when he heard the sound of pebbles striking the window. He looked out and saw Marie Lynn looking up at his window. "I'll get my shoes on and come out there," he whispered, "They don't let women visit after dark." When he got outside, Marie Lynn held out an official-looking document from the government. Holding it up to the light, he saw that it was a commendation of bravery. "On November 14, 1918, Private First Class Tomás Fontinot, USMC, had captured a German machine gun and turned it on attacking German soldiers, killing many of them and securing a hilltop until relief troops arrived. Subsequently," it went on, "PFC Fontinot died of his wounds."

"So that was it?" Lou asked Marie Lynn. "He got the silver star for valor—posthumously, of course. That's how they knew he was a Cajun." Lou looked at Marie Lynn with something between a smile and a grimace, and she nodded.

"It was three days after the war was over," she said quietly. "Does that signify it don't mean nothing?"

Lou thought for a few minutes and then shook his head. "I don't think so," he said. He opened his arms to Marie Lynn, and she gripped him tightly and cried hard into his chest. When she had calmed a little, she said, "He saw through all the politics and the lies and that flag shit, don't you think, brother?"

He nodded. "That's what I would expect. Tomás was too smart to believe that."

Smiling through her tears, she added, "And I expect our Tomás just done it for the hell of it, don't you think, brother?"

They stood for a long time holding onto each other. Finally, Lou said, "There's a fishing tackle place out on the edge of town that stays open all night. What say we go get us some breakfast?"

"Are you sure about what he believed?" she asked.

After a moment, he shook his head. "No," he said, "but I know he wouldn't have wanted us to miss breakfast."

Over breakfast, Marie Lynn grew serious again. "Louis," she said, "if you or I have sons, promise me you'll help me raise them so they don't throw their lives away like Tomás did." Lou smiled. "I'm glad to promise you that, dear sister, but I don't think anybody could have talked me or Tomás out of it either."

"Yeah, but you've been there and seen it now. You and Tomás didn't have nobody to tell you, with Daddy being dead and all."

"I hope you're right, Marie Lynn. It would sure gratify me if you were."

At Lou's urging, and with what financial help he could manage, Marie Lynn finished high school in Natchitoches—the first in the family to do so; and eventually, she was able to find a job at the college library. She shared Lou's pleasure in books, and in the quiet lives they both lived, a highlight for brother and sister was to spend Sunday afternoon after church talking about whatever they were reading at the time.

They both used to laugh at the thought that as Cajuns, they were secret readers; and that as a librarian, Marie Lynn was a even a secret Cajun. Not being married and their mother having long since passed on, Marie Lynn used her free time to begin taking courses at the Louisiana State Normal College in Natchitoches, where she was working now as an assistant librarian. In the beginning, she just took courses whenever she could fit them into her work schedule. After a few years, she was able to rearrange her work schedule to accommodate the courses she still needed to complete a bachelor of arts degree in library science.

To her own surprise, she graduated in 1929 ("Causing the stock market to crash," she always joked because she said it must certainly have been a terrible shock to the universe for a Fontinot to go to college, much less finish). Eventually, she quietly married her long-time boyfriend, Kyle McCall, who taught English at the high school in Natchitoches near the main campus of the college.

Earlier, Lou had found a place called the EZ Duzit outside Natchitoches, between Alexandria and Shreveport. Soon, he had struck up a kind of joking, flirting friendship with a woman named Annie, who bartended at the speakeasy and was saving her money—having made an agreement with the widow woman who owned the place that would enable her eventually to buy it outright. Soon, Annie and Louis began "keeping company," as the saying went. Finally, Annie invited him to stay one night—in a way that seemed comfortably natural—and they drifted into a quiet, friendly domesticity.

One night in 1925, Annie told him she was pregnant. He asked if he was the father, and she said he was. The story he told later was that he said, "Well hell, I never tried being married before. Let's do it." The way Annie told it, he said, "What you want to do about it?" To which she replied, "What do you think, you big bastard?" They were married at the EZ Duzit and went on honeymoon to Baton Rouge in his Model T Ford.

A little east of Lafayette, deep in Cajun country, they came upon a roadside place covered with signs, saying things like "See live snakes and alligators." "See 'Swamper Boudreau' wrestle a 'gator to the death."

"I heard about those," Annie called over the wind and engine noise. "I heard they was all fake."

"Probably," Lou called back, but they stopped anyway. Once inside, they looked around and decided it wasn't much, but Lou sensed right away he had found his ticket.

In the hotel in Baton Rouge that night, he told her, "I think I'd like to go somewhere around Shreveport and open me up one of them alligator places."

"With what?" Annie asked derisively. "And why Shreveport?"

"I got a little something put away," he replied, "and I can probably get my family to help me get some 'gators and maybe some snakes and stuff. And maybe that far north, I could pass as a true Cajun."

"And who's going to wrestle them?"

"Well, me maybe." At that, she laughed again; and to keep from sounding too full of himself, he added, "And maybe I can hire somebody too."

"Well, don't quit your day job yet, honey, 'cause you're going to be feeding three of us pretty soon."

Three months later, Annie miscarried. They flushed the fetus down the toilet, and Annie went to bed and cried. Lou felt useless. He asked her what he could do to help, but she would only say, "Nothing."

"I'm really sorry, Annie," he said.

"Sure."

"Please let me help you some way. I really am so sorry that you lost your baby."

She did not say anything for a while. Lou sat quietly by the bed, gazing down at his hands clasped between his knees. Finally, Annie took a deep breath and said softly, "You don't feel a goddamned thing, do you?"

"Well, of course I do," he protested.

"No. I understand what you're saying. I ain't saying you don't care what happens to me. I know you don't want me to be sad or anything—because you might have to look at me some new way. I'm talking about the baby. 'Is it my baby?' you had the balls to ask. No, it belongs to the goddamned man in the moon. You never wanted that little piece of human in the first place, and you never knew enough of who I really am to know whether you wanted *me* or not."

Lou tried without success to find a suitable reply; and she went on implacably, as though talking to herself, "That baby died for lack of being wanted."

"Oh, come on, Annie."

"Don't 'Come on, Annie' me," she shouted suddenly. "I know you, you goddamned drunk. You and your fucking books and your fucking moonshine. What do you think, you bastard? When did you ever love anything or anybody? Don't argue with me. I don't want to talk to you anymore. I don't want to see your damned sad face anymore. I don't want to smell your stinking booze anymore. I'm sick, do you hear me? I'm wore out. I lost my fucking baby, goddamn you. All I wanted was a little love—and that baby. I wish you would just go off somewhere and crawl under something and fucking die."

The next day, Lou paid up the rent for another month and moved his belongings to a boarding house in Shreveport.

Marie Lynn came to visit one Sunday after he got settled, and they walked out to the little park behind his boarding house. "You ever try to figure out how we're going to turn out, brother?" she asked half seriously.

He laughed richly. "When I want to scare myself."

The two of them fell silent for a while. "How about you?" Lou asked presently.

Marie Lynn looked at him straight on until he dropped his eyes. "I think, in a way, it's too bad we're family. We might have made a good couple." That was the only time they went near that particular subject. Lou came to enjoy his brother-in-law's company. As a teacher, Kyle took a kind of avuncular interest in his students, very few of whom shared his pleasure in the literature he taught. But that didn't prevent Kyle from being amused by them or from collecting what he considered their "priceless observations on life."

Kyle and Marie Lynn were the only other people Lou knew who enjoyed talking about books. The three of them saw themselves a kind of cabal tucked away in the fastness of west central Louisiana and laughingly referred to themselves as the three musketeers.

"But one thing I don't get," Kyle said to Lou one night on the far side of a couple of bottles of wine, "Marie Lynn's the librarian, I'm the lit teacher. But who the hell are you?" Lou thought for a minute and offered, "I guess I'm the 'secret sharer,' masquerading as an alligator wrestler." Kyle was delighted and told Marie Lynn that Lou had become a fan of Joseph Conrad.

A few years later, when Marie Lynn delivered her only child, Lou was the first family member to arrive at the hospital, energetically shaking Kyle's hand and solemnly holding and rocking his new nephew.

"So what's this young man's name?" Lou asked. Kyle and Marie Lynn exchanged a quick look, and Marie Lynn nodded with a smile.

Kyle cleared his throat. "We were thinking about Tomás Marlow McCall," he said. "Tomás Marlow," Lou repeated. "Man!" he said, his throat scratchy. "I love the Tomás," he said, "but what about Marlow? I mean I love Conrad and all, but which Marlow are we talking about *Heart of Darkness* or alter egos or what?"

Marie Lynn smiled at him gently. "What do you think, brother?"

He looked at her continuing mysterious smile and honestly didn't know what she meant. "But maybe," she said, "with someone you love, just the feel of a shared mystery is enough."

"Well then, in that case, I guess I'm entirely speechless," he finally said. He gazed at the floor for a long time, feeling his way into it and hoping for inspiration. Finally he said reverently, "I'll try to live up to the honor."

Sometimes it's kinder to leave even those you love with the illusion that you have understood them—and to satisfy yourself with loving curiosity.

Kyle quietly noticed the look his wife and her brother exchanged. When Lou finally stood up to go home, Kyle put his arm around Marie Lynn and walked with her out into the moonlight to see Lou off. As Lou disappeared into the dark, Kyle said, "It's a good thing I'm not a jealous man." She studied him with care as though taking soundings on the depth of his meaning. Finally, she touched his cheek and softened her voice and said, "I'm grateful that you're not because I wouldn't want to lose you as my husband or as Marlow's father, either one."

Alligator Hides

> *Fear discloses an ineluctable potential for loss; and so it confronts the child with desire as contradiction ... Fear inspires futures that [the child] has already perceived to be intrinsically uncertain. In fear, and perhaps out of fear, we make a future we also cannot afford to believe in.*[8]
>
> —Adam Phillips, *Terrors and Experts*

Louis Fontinot sits at the big kitchen worktable after the breakfast rush in his café, cleaning an industrial-grade gas burner. With extraordinary concentration, he presses a stiff wire into one gas hole after another, extracting from each a tiny plug of carbon black and grease. Occasionally, he gives a proprietary glance around the ample commercial kitchen, with its red brick floor and stainless steel tabletops, sinks, and counters.

He raises his head, alert and listening. Across the table from him, a woman dressed in jeans and a T-shirt sets down her coffee cup and appears to listen intently too. She is Elvira Jackson—slender, black, and a decade younger than Louis. He drops the wire onto the tabletop, still concentrating. The only sounds coming through the open windows are bird calls and the sporadic rustling of tree leaves. Leaf shadows create the momentary illusion of camouflage moving across the hands, arms, faces, and torsos of the two listeners.

"You hear from Marlow yet?" Elvira asks quietly. Lou shakes his head.

"*She* still here?" Elvira whispers.

He nods.

"My sweet Lord Jesus! What you got yourself into now?"

He shakes his head.

[8.] Adam Phillips, *Terrors and Experts* (Cambridge, Mass.: Harvard University Press, 1995), 52-53.

"Where'd she spend the night? Your room?"

Grimacing shamefacedly, he nods. "I slept in the office," he says quickly.

"Umm. Umm. Umm," she chants. "Where her husband at?"

"She said she left him. Looks like she's running from something."

Elvira perches on her high stool by the table, morosely sipping coffee. "How I'm supposed to watch out for you and you be such a fool?"

He doesn't answer.

Later, having finished cleaning the burner, Louis makes his way out the back door to a grove of pecan trees behind the café. Ten tourist cabins, freshly painted white with dark green trim, enclose the grove in a horseshoe. The nearest cabin is bigger than the others. A sign on the door identifies it as the office.

Louis enters the cabin and straightens some magazines scattered on a coffee table and couch. He checks the guest register on the counter and finds "Lillian Stallings, Houston" written on the top line in ragged letters. He tears the page from the register and puts it into his pocket. A door behind the counter is marked "Louis Fontinot, Manager."

As he starts through the door, the bell on the front door jangles, and a young man of eighteen pushes through.

Louis looks up warily. "Where you been?"

"Sorry, Uncle Lou," the boy says. "I should've called or something."

"Your mother called for you last week. She said you were upset about something and wouldn't tell her what. She said you might not be coming back to work."

"Yeah, well. I'm sorry. I shouldn't have just not showed up like that." The boy hooks his thumbs into the pockets of his jeans and pushes his shoulders up. At length, he blurts out so quickly, his voice cracks, "Yeah, well, do you still want me to work or what?"

Louis studies him for several breaths. When he answers, his voice has softened, "Sure I want you to work. What do you mean? Do we need to talk about something?"

"Yeah. I guess so. But . . ."

"Let's go outside then, Marlow," Lou says jovially, "and like they say, set a spell and see if we can think of something that'll make any kind of sense." Marlow mumbles his thanks and follows his uncle back out the door to a shady pecan grove. Dark green picnic tables with benches and other heavy lawn furniture made of thick wood sit solidly under the trees. Lou drops down onto a bench at one of the tables, inhaling appreciatively and slowly exhaling. A water sprinkler with heavy three-foot brass arms turns lazily in the shade, slinging thick ropes of water onto the grass, cooling the air. The initials "JB" and "Ruthie" and "BJ+Tim" are carved deeply into the top of the table where Louis sits. Many coats of paint have left the surfaces glassy and the deeply carved initials rounded at the edges. Marlow perches on the bench across the table from him.

"Okay," says Louis, "I haven't laid eyes on you since the night that little incident took place last week, so I'm speculating this has something to do with that. Right?"

The boy nods. "Yes, sir," he says stiffly.

Lou nods back, as though in agreement. "Okay, son, you want to just tell me? I'm guessing you got your feelings hurt or you're worried or something. But you're not going to hurt my feelings."

"Well, sir, I wouldn't quite say my feelings were hurt . . ."

"So how would you put it?"

"I feel stupid saying this, but I guess . . . I mean what I thought at the time was that I didn't know what to make of it. I hadn't ever seen you do anything like that, and I couldn't imagine why you did it. Then I wondered if you *knew* her or something. It was really a turn-on at first," he says sheepishly, blushing. "But then almost immediately, I felt dirty just standing there watching. I had seen you pouring the whisky into her coffee and couldn't figure it out. I don't mean anything against you, Uncle Lou. It was just me, feeling dirty for enjoying it."

Marlow falls silent, and Lou taps pensively on the tabletop. The sprinkler seems loud in the background. Traffic noise begins to intrude from the nearby road. Finally, Lou chuckles and shakes his head. Marlow looks up, surprised. "I'm not laughing at you, son. I'm laughing at myself. I've been asking myself the same questions, and maybe feeling some of that same dirtiness you mentioned."

Lou laughs again. He rubs his face, gets out his handkerchief, blows his nose, and carefully puts his handkerchief away. "Goddamn it, Marlow," he says.

Marlow raises his head and straightens his back. His pupils begin to dilate, and he grows watchful.

"You know," Lou continues, "I hate like a son of a bitch being in the wrong. And if there's anything I hate more than being wrong, it's having to admit it."

"Uncle Lou . . ." Marlow protests, making a gesture that looks like pushing the air with his open palm as though warding off a blow.

"No, Marlow, it's not just you. Elvira's been taking the hide off of me for a week now. She's got you beat all to hell when it comes to pointing out the errors of my ways." He grins at Marlow then frowns at the grass. "Seriously, son, it was a shameful performance, and I'm sorry and embarrassed you had to see it."

Marlow stands up abruptly, accidentally knocking over his bench, but Lou preempts him. "But wait till you hear the latest." Marlow stops. "The lady has come back."

"She what?" Marlow looks incredulous. Lou stifles a smile, thinking he might just as well have told the kid that the pecan trees had started walking.

"Here, I'll give you a hand with that," Lou says, reaching for the overturned bench.

"What? Oh, thanks," Marlow says, reaching down.

The woman who signed in as Lillian Stallings has been asleep in Lou's cabin, dressed in a khaki work shirt, her dark hair rumpled. She vaguely recalls the cabins and the pecan grove from the night a few days ago when she and her husband stopped for coffee at the café at two in the morning on their way to Florida, but she cannot piece together what she is doing here now.

She feels trapped in the distortions of a dream that could turn horrific at any moment. The fear grows from a week-old memory of slamming out of a front door, vomiting into some bushes bordering the parking lot, then wrenching open the car door and sitting down inside to wait for her husband, Gerald.

But now, groggy with fatigue and too little sleep, she can't remember why. Her hair feels matted. Her fingers hurt. Her face feels raw and chapped, and judging from her body odor, she suspects that she has not bathed in several days. A knock sounds on the door, and she grimaces. "Oh, not yet," she mumbles, sitting up and placing her feet carefully on the floor. She stands shakily then pads barefoot to the door. She clears her throat and manages to ask hoarsely, "Who is it?"

From outside, Louis calls, "Ms. Stallings?" and asks if he can come in.

Hesitantly, Lillian replies, "Just a second." A cursory look down at herself reveals the unfamiliar shirt, which falls modestly to her knees; though to her dismay, she has no memory of putting it on. She fastens the chain and cracks open the door. "Yes?"

"How you feeling?" Lou asks softly from outside.

Lillian removes the chain. "Where are my clothes?"

"Hanging in the bathroom. They should be about dry."

Unintentionally, Lillian has automatically taken the chain off the latch, and as she walks to the bathroom, Lou steps inside. Returning, she stops suddenly when she sees that he is inside the room. She swallows with a dry throat. "I don't know your name," she says, backing up.

"Lou Fontinot." Without thinking, he holds out his hand, but when she doesn't move, he withdraws it awkwardly.

"I'm Lillian Stallings," she says firmly. "Who washed my clothes?"

Lou shrugs and grins self-consciously, his permanent sunburn deepening. His face is lumpy, with scar tissue along the eyebrow ridges, and his nose is more misshapen than she remembered.

"*You* did?" Lillian asks.

Lou nods.

"Underwear too?"

The desperate rictus is now etched into his face as he mumbles a nerveless, "Yep."

Now she too blushes. "Must have been gross," she mutters. She thinks for a moment, then asks, "Where's my car?"

"My garage," Lou replies. "Your keys are on the dresser there."

Lillian glances at the dresser. "Thank you," she says finally. "It's important nobody sees the tags."

"It was pretty late when you got here. I doubt anybody noticed it." Lou pauses. The hand he wipes across his face is gnarled and sunburned. "Look," he says, his eyes on the floor, "I apologize for the other night."

"Sure," Lillian says, hardly daring to try remembering, "but could I have a shower and get dressed before we talk about that?"

"Oh, of course," he says, fairly dancing with relief at the subject change. "Get your purse and stuff, and I'll walk you over to your cabin."

Uncomprehending, Lillian follows Lou out the front door and watches while he unlocks the next cabin over. He enters, opens windows, turns on the ceiling fan, and checks the bathroom. "How did I get a cabin?" Lillian asks, frowning.

"The woman who works with me put out a clean towel and things," Lou says. "Cabin was her suggestion. We have plenty of room. Make yourself as comfortable as you can. Her name is Elvira, by the way. We'll probably see her in the café."

Lillian blanches. "The café?"

"You remember . . ." Lou stops, flustered.

"Of course," Lillian says, averting her eyes to avoid her own embarrassment as well as his. Finally, she takes a deep breath and says, "Look . . ." She peers at him. "I don't quite know how to say this," she begins. "Don't jump to any conclusions, you know?"

Perplexed, Lou nods vigorously, as though to encourage her.

"Well, it's just that no matter what you did . . . I'm still not clear on that beyond knowing it was outrageous, okay?" Lou nods and swallows. "So I'm not just blowing that off. I may want to return to that later, but I can't . . ." Lillian takes a deep breath and changes direction. "What I mean is that's not why I'm here, you see, and I owe it to you to warn you that I may be just a little . . . you know . . . crazy." She *barks* an oversized laugh. "So no doubt you're thinking, 'Otherwise she wouldn't be here.' Right?" She laughs again, then compresses her lips as if to prevent herself from laughing too much. Or to keep the lips from cracking from dryness.

"I still don't want to get into all that about the other night right now," she continues. Lou nods again. "It's just that when we were visiting our new granddaughter in Florida, my husband and daughter and son-in-law began patronizing me . . . See, I'm just thirty-eight years old, and my nineteen-year-old daughter just had a baby, same age as me when I had her. You see? So it's like they're afraid this little old thirty-eight-year-old grandmother might . . . What is it you say? 'Go off her trolley?' Or not know how to act?"

Lou nods hopefully. "Got it," he says.

"Worse than that . . ."

Lillian stops and looks down at her feet, which Lou notices now are scratched, their nail polish mostly worn off.

When Lillian speaks again, her voice breaks and she stops again and starts over. "They seemed not to trust me to hold my granddaughter, you know?"

Unable to speak, she pauses to swallow again before going on. "I do some weird things sometimes, but . . ."

She stands up straight and takes a deep breath. "Okay. Enough," she says out loud, but addressed to herself. "Enough for now. What it comes down to is, please don't be afraid of me, Mr. Fontinot." She looks at him imploringly.

"You see," she continues doggedly, "Just recently, something has happened. It's just that I keep suddenly feeling that a person I'm talking to—like to you right now—is suddenly growing very small and far away, like at the wrong end of a telescope?" She checks Lou for a reply and he nods. "It scares me to death. That's all. Okay?"

"Got it," Lou repeats quietly. "Get showered, and I'll bring you a breakfast tray in thirty minutes."

"Make it an hour?"

"Done. Here's your room key. Please lock yourself in."

"*Why?*" Lillian almost screams.

Lou laughs and says, "To keep you from thinking I'm going to break in on you. That's what Elvira said."

She digests this and asks, "Then I am free to leave?"

He laughs. "Whenever you want to, but I don't want you to think you're not welcome, and I think you need some rest before you try to drive."

Lillian's shoulders, having felt as though they were hunched clear up to her ears, now seem to be settling down an inch or so and she smiles.

"And by the way," he adds, "please call me Lou."

After Lou is gone, Lillian locks the door. She drops the shirt to the floor and walks into the bathroom. Her nakedness feels strange to her, but not unpleasant. The woman who works for him, Elvira (she smiles at the old timey name), has left her a towel and wash cloth as well as a comb, soap, hand lotion, and shampoo, and even a new toothbrush and a little tube of toothpaste. She smiles and turns the hot water on hard as it will go.

Her hair hangs down to her shoulders. She soaps it luxuriously for a long time, and while the water pours down over her face and body, she revels in the feeling. Her eyes still closed, she sees the vision again of her daughter Cindy gentling the new baby with a murmur and a caress, efficiently changing her and deftly scooping her up again and disposing of the wet diaper.

Ignoring Lillian, Cindy hands the baby to Lillian's husband Gerald to hold. Lillian swallows back a sob before it can become audible. Just turned nineteen, Cindy could have passed for a veteran mother. Lillian holds her face up to the hot water and feels the flow but still relives standing in Cindy's bedroom, thinking, *She's exactly the same age I was when I had her. But where did she get all her confidence and poise? Dear God, I envy her easy tenderness!*

By the time Lou returns, Lillian is fresh and clean in her own slightly damp clothes. Her damp hair is combed and hangs down around her face. She is sitting cross-legged on the floor, rubbing hand cream into her pale, ravaged fingers and cuticles. She gets up to let him in, and he sets the tray beside her. She looks at the eggs, bacon, orange juice, coffee, and little sweet rolls and butter—surprised to realize that she is hungry. Delicately, she touches the cloth napkin, the silverware, and the china sugar bowl and creamer.

Lou has been watching her. He rouses himself and says, "Say, why don't we take this out to one of the picnic tables?"

"I don't know," Lillian says. "This feels pretty safe right here. What about the other guests?"

"Just one cabin and they're out now. Anyway, they're just three college kids here for some kind of meeting. Very quiet and polite."

In the pecan grove, the lazy sprinkler has been turned off, but water still sparkles on the dark, stiff St. Augustine grass blades. "Nice," Lillian says, nodding—a habit a student recently told her makes her appear to be agreeing with herself.

"You feel safe enough?" Lou asks.

"Well, yes, since Elvira told you not to break down my door," Lillian says, smiling. "These tables and benches look like they've been here for a while," she says, presently. "And solid. Well worn but solid. How long have you been here anyway? Gerald wondered about that when we were here before, you know?" She pauses, surprised at what she is saying and remembering.

She is not accustomed to speaking so freely with strangers, particularly about herself. "You told him you were in the First World War. Was that war just endless horror? I mean, in the trenches and all. Gerald was in the Second World War, but he just flew an airplane, and he crashed it anyway. I'm talking too much, I know, but it feels so damned good to feel safe."

"I moved to Shreveport in 1927," Lou says matter-of-factly.

"Wow," she says, "that's over thirty years! Twenty-seven from sixty—thirty-three years! And your wife?"

Lou hesitates, clears his throat, and finally says, "I moved here when we separated."

"Sorry," she says meekly. "I was out of bounds."

They sit quietly while she eats. Finally, she pushes the tray away—careful of her fingers—and says, "Okay, I've got to ask this—all right? So here goes . . ." Her mouth keeps filling with saliva, and she swallows again.

"So all that alligator stuff I saw in the café, the other night . . . ?" She stops again, not quite comprehending where these memories and this rush to talk are coming from. "I mean, those hides and pictures and all that. What's that all about?"

He laughs. "That was my meal ticket for thirty years."

She shakes her head. "But alligators?"

Still laughing, Lou says, "Annie and me . . . that was my wife. We drove over to New Orleans for a sort of honeymoon one time, and we passed a place on the road that caught my attention. So on the way back, we stopped in and talked to the guy, and it just sort of come to me that a reptile zoo was maybe something I could do to make a living."

"But why?" she repeats.

"Who knows? My nephews down in Lafayette are real Cajuns. They supply the reptiles, and I was sick and tired of getting my face busted for a living . . . which is what I had been doing—a little prize fighting, doing security, that kind of thing." He stops and smiles at her. "Maybe this talking to strangers is contagious," he says.

Lou studies his hands until she decides he is not going to say anything more, but then he adds, "If you don't mind my mentioning it though, what the hell brings you here after I done what I done the other night in front of all them people? Or even if I had been a perfect gentleman far as that goes? You don't know me."

Lillian purses her lips but does not speak.

Quickly, Lou adds, "Don't get me wrong. I like having you here. I just can't imagine how bad it must have got at your daughter's house to drive you over what? Seven hundred miles of bad road? To *here* of all places . . ." His voice trails off. "I know that's none of my business."

"No." Lillian shakes her head. "It's reasonable," she says, smiling. "I'm just not sure I know the answers."

She closes her eyes and continues to sit. She remembers standing in Cindy's kitchen, eavesdropping on a conversation between Gerald, Cindy, and Cindy's husband Robert on the back stairs at their little house. Robert's voice carried up to her clearly.

"Look, I don't want in on this." She remembers him saying, or something like that. "Leave me completely out of the decision making. But I'll be glad to drive over to campus this morning and call around. Maybe get hold of somebody in the psych department. Probably find somebody in Gainesville to see her. Maybe the hospital there. I doubt she needs a sanitarium or anything like that. Probably just a hospital for a day or two to get herself oriented."

Lillian remembers back to herself shivering as a cold chill passed down her back and belly simultaneously. She clenched her teeth against the cold; and then she just got clear, almost unbearably alert, heart thundering in her chest as she scanned the strange environment for clues to tell her what to do next. Then the baby started crying in the bedroom.

As she shakes her head clear of the memory, Lillian's eyes implore Lou's. "It was like I had to escape from the police or something. Not really, but that's how it felt. I picked up my purse and the car keys. Gerald just gaped at me until I asked him for the gasoline card. I told him I would fill up the tank while I was out, that I needed to pick up some women's things at a drugstore we had passed on the way in the day before."

She pauses, remembering. "And he was like a sleepwalker, you know? Like he had no volition. He just pulled out his billfold, although he didn't look happy. I kept expecting him to balk, but he just pulled out the card and handed it to me. I said to myself, 'Thank you, God,' and slipped the card into my purse and eased out the door before any of them could say, 'Boo!'

"Then I just ran like a rabbit and kept on running—kept getting lost. I don't rightly know how many days. I had some personal problems along the way that I can't talk about now—until I finally wound up here. I've been missing now for several days, and I assume Gerald has had time to recover his ability to react.

"I hope this doesn't hurt your feelings, uh, Lou," she continues levelly. "But, sad to say, I couldn't think of any other place to turn to, not to mention the plain fact that probably it was the *last* place anybody would look for me."

After a pause, she smiled at him. "And without realizing it at the time, I guess I thought you owed me one, even if I still can't quite remember why."

In their intensity, they have leaned side by side on one of the heavy green picnic tables. Lou looks carefully at their contrasting hands. Finally, he says, "Now I have to tell you the real reason I chose alligators." Lillian peers at him quizzically. "You know how hard those ridges are on their skin?"

She nods. "I guess. I mean, I can imagine that they must be hard."

"Well," he says, "in between the ridges, their skin is just soft as a puppy's nose."

Lillian raises her eyebrows at their two hands. It's clear that her thoughts are elsewhere. Finally, she stands up straight, nods, and murmurs absently, "That soft?"

Part Three
Fitting In

    The crucial breakthrough occurred for Prigogine during the early 1960's, when he realized that systems far from equilibrium must be described by nonlinear equations. The clear recognition of this link between "far from equilibrium" and "nonlinearity" opened an avenue of research for Prigogine that would culminate a decade later in his theory of self-organization.[9]

Fritjof Capra. The Web of Life

[9.] Fritjof Capra. The Web of Life: a new scientific understanding of living systems. (New York: Anchor Books) 1996, p. 86.

CIVIL DISOBEDIENCE

Bad laws are the worst sort of tyranny.[10]

—Edmund Burke, *Speech at the Guildhall in Bristol*

Too much was going on. Even though I knew better, I *felt* caught up in it and even a little drained as I walked back toward my cabin. That and the overlap from my lost week sort of ran together. I had forgotten about my fingers, but now that I concentrated on them, I hadn't realized the cuticles still hurt; although now that I checked, they were showing promise of healing, just a little tender to the touch. Tires crunched the shell on the road behind me. I was growing accustomed to that as the ordinary sound of passing vehicles.

As the car passed, freckled Edward leaned out of the open window and hollered, "See ya!" as they passed while the other two boys continued to sit, smile, and wave sedately. It was easy to imagine Edward twelve years ago without front teeth. I gave him back a big, wide wave for encouragement—though it felt forced—and then watched them turn right at the road, heading in the direction of the H-E-B supermarket. I thought of them as law-abiding boys, pretending not to be frightened even though I knew they expected—in just a few hours—to be purposely breaking laws they had been raised to respect.

They had just concluded a meeting at the picnic table in the pecan grove behind the café's kitchen. I had been enjoying the shade in the one of the chairs when Ralph and Charles, the first two boys, walked up. They sat down at the wooden picnic table and very politely introduced themselves. They looked to be about twenty or so, just two or three years older than my math

---

[10.] Edmund Burke, Speech at the Guildhall in Bristol (1780). In *The Works of the Right Honorable Edmund Burke*, Volume 2 (Boston: Little, Brown).

students at home and maybe a year older than my daughter. I found them awkwardly charming. We had made small talk for a while until Edward joined them and said they needed to get moving.

They more or less ignored me then as they continued to plan what turned out to be a "sit-in" that afternoon at the lunch counter of the H-E-B supermarket down the road. I thought of leaving, both to give them privacy and to protect my innocence, but I was intrigued by their discussion. Their job, they said, would be to reconnoiter the store to make sure nobody appeared to have been tipped off that the sit-in was imminent and that no police were on hand.

I wondered who had made the larger plan that assigned them these jobs. They planned, they said, to bring the car back here to the motel and leave it before the demonstration. Then this afternoon, about five twenty, after the other participants got off work or out of school, the three would return on foot from different directions. Each one would enter the store separately and order a soft drink or coffee and busy himself with schoolbooks. If it looked okay, at five twenty-five, Edward would stroll out the front door and "stretch his legs." That would be the signal to the fifteen or twenty mostly Negro members of the group to begin filtering in, shopping a little, then nonchalantly sitting down at the lunch counter and placing their orders. The boys hadn't told anyone other than the participants, fearing a leak, and also not wanting to incriminate anyone outside the group. And of course, they hadn't directly told me. At the moment, I secretly wished I had left before hearing about it. They were pretty tense as it was, and I wondered if any of them regretted having spoken in front of me.

Now I was remembering those feelings as I watched them until they disappeared around some buildings. Turning back, I was surprised to see Lou standing beside my door. I was surprised also at how comforting it felt to see him.

"Hey," he said. I felt like giving him a hug. "What you been up to?" he asked.

"Talking to the neighbors."

"I didn't know you were so sociable."

"Me either. These kids'll wear you out. They're so serious, you know? They make me feel drab and out of tune."

"Yeah? And what else?"

I turned to him and squinted against the sun, reluctant to answer. At length, I took a deep breath. "They're just a little older than my daughter," I said. His attentiveness had invited tears that raised the pitch of my voice and choked off the words. He looked at me closely but waited. "So I guess I see her in them, in a way," I continued.

"At their age, I was already a young mother and all, and I was thinking that Cindy will miss that time in her life too, being almost the same young mother that I was." I fell silent, not knowing quite what I wanted to say; and when I spoke again, there was a catch in my throat. "And I *miss* her," I blurted. Tears stopped me momentarily, but then I suddenly confided a non sequitur while laughing at myself. "I wish I had been a better mother," I said, realizing that I didn't really know Cindy that well and that now I wished I had looked at her more closely when she was growing up and wondered how she saw me.

Lou nodded as though he had known what I'd been thinking, even though there was no way he could have. "Never had a kid," he said surprisingly at last. "But I can imagine you missing her and worrying about how she feels. I was with my wife when she miscarried our baby, and I can remember how helpless and terrible that was." He smiled. "Even though I could never make her believe I cared." With difficulty, I focused on him. But when I did, the image of us sharing our separate sad memories moved me. I sat down in one of his office chairs and breathed for a while in the silence.

"Yeah," I told him eventually. "And you know, these kids who are staying at the motel are into so many things. One of them said this morning, 'Even though I'm white, the effects of discrimination are palpable to me.'" At his age, I wouldn't even have known the word. "Another one quoted Thoreau on what he called 'our moral duty to break unjust laws' or something like that. And they say anyway that they are ready to break bad laws and take the consequences."

"I wonder," Lou said, "if they know what they're saying."

"There's another thing. They say they have some colored members in their group who would have liked to stay here at the motel because it's so close to the store, but they were afraid you wouldn't rent them a room."

"Nobody has tried so far as I know."

"Would you if they had?"

As Lou thought that over, I tried to picture myself in his place. My oscillation between excitement and caution was paralyzing. "I don't know." Lou said eventually, echoing my feelings. "I wouldn't want to run off my other customers, but that's a pretty sorry excuse for not doing something you think is right."

It's realistic, though, I thought. "Would it be against the law in Louisiana to rent to blacks and whites staying in the same room?" I asked, feeling naïve.

"I don't think so." Lou repeated. "But mixed-race couples would be in real danger around here, and not just because of the Klan. I don't know what the 'good citizens' might do if I rented a room to two straight black men, much less to a male-female couple where one was white and the other one black. But I'd rather not bet the motel on either one being safe." He shook his head and laughed wryly. "Funny how much our peace of mind depends on our ability not to know something. I could have asked somebody before now."

He grinned crookedly. "If I knew who to ask."

"I get the impression that one—maybe two—of these kids have been taking it more seriously than we have," I said, "more like the old abolitionists did back in the day. Sort of like you and Marie Lynn, leading private, principled lives—in contrast to me, just sort of embracing it as the lark of the moment." The two of us studied each other's faces in silence for a while. The cicadas were starting up in the trees.

Then I straightened up, aware that the personal usually trumps the rest for me. "All I know is I would feel a lot better if Cindy didn't think I'm crazy, and I wonder if getting involved in civil rights demonstrations at my age counts as crazy." I grin up at him to dilute my self-drama, and he puts his hand on my cheek, which is wet. Then we began walking toward the cabins. I am surprised to find myself aroused.

An airplane was passing in the distance. Lou looked in the direction of the sound. "What does your husband think about all this civil rights stuff?" he asked.

"I don't know that he thinks about it. He's probably more riled up about the teach-ins against the Southeast Asian fighting, but I don't know that," I said. "He used to say he felt cheated because he never got to complete a combat mission during the war."

"If he had got to complete one, he'd probably know by now how un-cheated he was."

I was reluctant to ask him what he meant, so I kept the conversation on Gerald. "He doesn't say much of anything about any of that anymore, but I watch his face when the war news comes on television. It makes him like, intent, you know? But he never was one of those guys who march around with the American Legion. Oops, I hope you aren't either. Are you?"

Lou continued to ponder without commenting.

I looked at him carefully. "I never hear you say much about your war and all that."

He grinned ruefully. "Come on," I say, "I'm serious." I study his rough, disfigured face carefully for a couple of breaths and then continue. "I have come to be appalled at how few things I have taken seriously, especially talking to these kids."

He looked at me and started to say something but changed his mind. I felt my face burn as my mind dredged up all the old derogatory misogynist clichés I could have imagined him using at this point. Although he hadn't said any of them, it felt as though he had. I wondered if the sexist language and the manners are just a southern thing. Never having lived anywhere else, I had no way of knowing. I wondered if my not wanting to be a grandmother at thirty-eight was just vanity, or worse, a sign that without meaning to, I was buying into that same misogyny.

"Well," he says, finally returning to my question, "I don't think going to France gave my life any great meaning. I mean, I liked France and still miss it sometimes, especially the girls and the wine . . . and the food. But the rest of it was just hard work, and ugly sights and smells. And fear." He looks at the ground for a few moments, as though remembering. "And in the end, I lost my favorite brother." He looks at me as though searching. "You know?"

There! I heard *his* voice fail him, however briefly. "For no good reason that I could ever see. In a way, Tomás was France for me—everything pretty and graceful and sophisticated. So now, France and all the bullshit that went with it in my mind has come to stand for the sort of ugly world that is left since Tomás has been gone, or something like that."

Of course, I think. *Nice foot in the mouth, Lillian.* "I should already have known that," I hurry to say. "Don't know why I brought it up. I don't know why we're even talking about wars anyway. These kids aren't that patriotic. If anything, they talk about the government as their enemy, especially the sheriff and mayor and all the local politicians."

"But how about the civil rights stuff? Does the segregation and all those things they're complaining about bother you?"

He considered the question. "That's hard to say," he said with a laugh. "I've lived with that stuff so long it's hard to remember whether I was upset about it at their age or not. Probably so, but I guess I don't let it raise my temperature any more. It's like some of my folks getting bent out of shape over being put down as Cajuns."

I stopped and turned toward him, studying his face. Finally, without thinking, I touched his upper arm and told him, "You're pretty surprising. For an old man." He answered with his big, distancing laugh. "Yeah, I'm just softening you up so I can spike your coffee and fondle your breast in front of my customers."

He turned and headed off toward the kitchen with his surprisingly springy gait, and I started back across the pecan grove, feeling the accumulated tiredness from my week of hard living. I pictured myself sitting in the shade of the pecan trees on one of the heavy chairs and listening to the water sprinklers and the cicadas that are just emerging. The air smelled like water. Uninvited, the image reappeared of Lou's assault on me that first night I ever saw the café, and I was a little surprised to find that the original revulsion had faded.

Wishing I had something to read, I ran back across to the kitchen and put my head in at the door. Elvira was working at the big table. "Excuse me," I said, "I was looking for Mr. Fontinot."

At that point, Lou stepped out of the walk-in cooler. He looked at me quizzically and then at Elvira. His face flushed, and then he put on his best "southern manners" and said, "Miz Jackson, this is Miz Lillian Stallings, our new guest in Cabin 2. Miz Stallings, Miz Jackson is our cook and my all-round assistant."

Elvira smiled at me, gave Lou a look—and out of the corner of my eye—I saw her roll her eyes at him. It came to me that she knew all about the incident the night Gerald and I stopped at the café—and disapproved. Then she wiped her hands on her apron and said, "Glad to have you staying with us, Ms. Stallings. Please call me Elvira. I hope you're comfortable."

All at once, I felt silly. "Thank you," I began, and Elvira started to speak simultaneously, saying, "Can I get y . . ." while I was saying, "Pardon me for inter . . ." Suddenly, we both broke out laughing. Lou looked from one of us to the other, and he began his own roaring laugh. For a few seconds, all three of us were caught in peals of laughter. As we tried to regain control, each of us tried again to speak and failed hilariously.

Finally, I managed to say between breaths, "We sound like a scene out of a bad school play." From Elvira, I felt a lively receptivity. She opened her arms, and we hugged each other, still catching our breath. Lou tore off a paper towel and wiped his eyes. As we calmed down, Elvira asked, "You okay with first names?"

I replied, "Of course."

She looked up at the back door as Marlow came in.

"Y'all all right?" he asked seriously.

Lou said jokingly, "Maybe you should ask me tomorrow."

I crossed to Marlow, held out my hand, and said, "Hi. I'm Lillian, as if you didn't know. I just came in looking for a book."

He took my hand firmly and nodded. His handsome young face was relaxed and open.

Lou recovered and said, "There's some books of mine in the office. Let me show you." He walked to the outside door and held it for me. Once in the office, Lou grinned and said, "Well, now you've met Elvira."

"And Marlow," I added. "You seemed worried about my meeting them. And by the way, I remember Marlow from that first night. He was the only one besides you who looked me in the eye."

"Yeah. Marlow don't miss much. He was pretty pissed at me about that night."

"And Elvira?"

"Her too."

Lou pushed his hands down into the pockets of his khakis and pursed his lips. "I wasn't exactly worried. Mostly curious," he replied. He ushered me into the office, which I was surprised to find neatly lined with shelves of books. "Help yourself," he said, then he gestured toward a small wooden 3x5 card file on the corner of his desk. "If you don't mind, I'd appreciate it if you would jot down the titles of whatever you borrow. My sister's a librarian, and she sort of looks after my books." Although he was smiling, I had a feeling that he was serious.

I smiled back at him and remarked, "You seem to have plenty of women looking after you."

"Yeah, well. I've heard nature hates a vacuum, whatever that means. Make yourself comfortable in here if you want to. I have to get back to work in the kitchen. Just pull the door shut when you leave if you don't mind. It locks itself."

As he turned to go, a siren sounded. We glanced out at the road and saw the sheriff's car rush by, followed by a highway patrol car.

"Your friends?" Lou asked.

"I'm afraid it could be. They were getting ready to do some kind of 'civil disobedience' as they called it. I think Marlow may be with them."

The sirens had stopped not too far down the road. Lou said, "I better go check on 'em."

"Could I go with you?" I asked almost shyly.

Lou looked at me and said, "I wouldn't." That diminished feeling again. (*Don't worry your pretty head, little lady.*)

"But those kids are my friends. They're sort of the same as my students."

Lou shook his head. "Anybody from this side of Louisiana would know you aren't from Shreveport, even if you did grow up in Texas. You been away too long, and I don't expect you want to show up on national TV right now for your husband to spot you on the news."

I shook my head reluctantly and turned back toward his office. I picked up a book almost at random, signed for it, and went back over to the café. There weren't many customers. I asked Elvira if she had heard the sheriff's car. She said, "Yeah, but I don't expect anything big going to happen tonight."

"Won't they take them to jail?"

"Might, but it won't amount to much. The Klans might do something in a day or two, but it'll be something sneaky. They could hang somebody, but more like they kill somebody's dog or something. They ain't going to do it out in the open. They might rape some housekeeper or something. That's more they style."

"I don't know," I said. "I wouldn't want to be the dog—or the housekeeper."

I went back outside. It was beginning to get dark. I couldn't hear anything coming from the H-E-B. I walked stealthily out to the road, keeping to the shadows. Looking to my right, I saw two more cars from the sheriff's department. A highway patrol car and a few private cars and a fire engine were parked here and there.

I crossed the road and made my way past the drugstore, which was closed, but its shadow gave me cover in a doorway. I looked out as individual people came and went. A small crowd of nonuniformed white men crowded around the front door of the supermarket, peering inside. Now I could hear voices from inside but couldn't tell what they were saying.

As I was craning my neck to try to see something, I looked back toward the road and saw someone walking up behind me. I stiffened until I saw that it was Elvira, as stealthy as I was. She came up beside me and said in a low voice that I shouldn't be there. I told her I knew that, but I couldn't stand the suspense. I also told her that it would be better for me to be seen there than her. She said, at least people knew who she was and that she wasn't an outside agitator.

I pulled her back into the shadow beside me, and we stood together a few more minutes; and suddenly, there was an eruption of noise from inside the store, and the crowd around the front door began to push and scramble around. Some of the white men standing outside ran into the building, and about then, I heard screams and shouts and the sound of furniture falling. Some black people tried to run out the door, but the white men at the front pushed and beat them back inside.

From up the road came two school buses. They pulled into the H-E-B parking lot and shut down and cut off the lights. One of the drivers got out and walked over to the front door. About that time, some of the deputies began moving the crowd of white men back from the door and telling them to go home. The deputies sounded friendly and didn't beat anybody. Some of the white men who had rushed inside now came back out, talking excitedly to the other men who crowded around them, and I noticed more cars driving up and more white men jumping out of them and running to join the crowd.

Then suddenly out of nowhere, I saw the large silhouetted shape of Lou rushing up to the door. He talked emphatically to the deputies in the door, saying that he needed to talk to the sheriff. Finally they allowed him to pass; and about that time, the deputies began roughly leading black people out of the store and loading them, men onto one bus and women onto the other. Each person was in handcuffs and had at least one deputy holding him or her by the elbow. It was hard to tell in the dark, but some of them appeared to have dark stains on their clothes. I asked Elvira if that was blood on them, and she nodded and said, "Probably."

The next thing that happened was that an ambulance pulled up, and the driver went inside and came back out and got on his radio; and his assistant, or whatever he was, jumped out and started getting a stretcher out of the back of the ambulance. Then the sound of sirens started in the distance. With the extra vehicles and so many people milling around, I stepped back to the drugstore and sort of hugged the wall to keep out of sight. Elvira moved up close enough to the front doors to see a little way inside.

We heard Lou yelling inside; and then to our great relief, he came out, walking really fast, leading Marlow and the other three boys and warning them not to run and to keep their eyes down. They passed by without noticing us, and we followed them because they were heading back toward the motel anyway. Several times, one or the other of the boys started talking; and each time, Lou told him to wait until we were all in the café kitchen. Then he turned around and saw me and Elvira and said, "What the hell are you two doing out here?" Then he laughed and hugged Elvira. Then he looked at me seriously for a minute and gave me a hug. It was the first time he had touched me since the night of the "incident," and I have to admit, it felt reassuring.

The kitchen was full of excited people—Lou, the boys, and Elvira and me all chattering. But Marlow spoke up and waited until everybody quieted a little and said, "Excuse me." He repeated himself. Finally, when we were quiet, he said, "I don't want to worry you all, but I have to go get on one of those buses."

There was a brief babble as he turned toward the door. Then Lou went to him and leaned in close. "Wait, son," he said. "What are you doing? Let's talk."

Marlow shook his head. "I have already thought it over, Uncle Lou. I'm sorry, but I have to get out there before they leave."

"Then I'll walk with you," Lou said. He told the other boys to "stay put." Then he turned to Marlow and said, "Come on." He walked out the door, with Marlow catching up to him. The rest of us stood and stared after them. The other boys conferred but, in the end, didn't move. A few minutes later, the two buses started up and moved off. The ambulance left, and another one took its place.

When Lou returned by himself, he looked at the boys and said, "I want you fellows to go back to your room until it's full daylight in the morning. Maybe you might ask Elvira to get you something to eat first, and you can take it to your room.

"But soon as it's daylight, it will be a good idea for you to drive straight home. Don't stop. Don't visit nobody. Whatever you do, don't give any interviews. The reporters are thick out there. I know publicity is what this is all about, but it needs to be organized and done by the leaders."

Eddie said, "We're supposed to meet with our organizers tomorrow in Natchitoches."

Lou said, "Then do it and let them take over. But for the next few days, try to stay out of sight, and don't go nowhere alone. There could be some sort of retaliation tomorrow or the next day. Y'all stirred them up good, and they *will* have some kind of revenge."

They said a chorus of "Yes sirs." "Elvira," Lou said, "Do you think anybody saw you and Lillian?"

"I don't think so."

"Okay," he said. "Here's what I need. I would like for you to find some place safe and out of sight where you can keep an eye on the motel and close to a phone, so you can call the sheriff if you see anybody breaking and entering. Is the kitchen the best, or is it the dining room?"

"I don't know," Elvira said. "Probably the dining room. Where you going to be?"

"Right now," he said," I'm going over to the jail to keep an eye on what they're doing. I already called Marlow's parents, and they are driving over now from Natchitoches. They may come here. I expect one of them will stay at the jail until Marlow gets out. I'll let you know as soon as I know something or he gets out. Stay close to the phone."

Elvira nodded and said, "I already got a pot of coffee on. Let me put it in a thermos for you."

"Thanks," Lou said. He turned and looked at me. "How you doing?"

"Okay. Worried about Marlow. Where is he?"

"He's on his way to the jail. Said he didn't want to get off any easier than the rest. You may want to be close to a phone tonight too. You can sleep in my room or the office."

I nodded, surprised and maybe frightened. "Sure," I said, "but why?"

"If I hear the cops are thinking of searching this place, you'll need to move your car to Marie Lynn's in Natchitoches. Get her address and a key to their house from Elvira. I wouldn't move it right now if you can help it because the cops are all over the place too. Your out-of-state license might spook 'em, and we don't need that. Okay?"

I nodded again, unable to think of anything appropriate to say.

He looked at Elvira and raised his eyebrows. "Get out of here," said Elvira. "Coffee's on the counter."

Lou left, and Elvira turned to the boys and asked "Y'all hungry?" They nodded enthusiastically. "Okay, while I put together some supper for you, Lillian and me would like to hear what started the trouble in there."

Edward, still playing leader, spoke right up. "Well," he said, "there was some argument about that. All I know is there was already a bunch of deputies and patrols in the store. They'd been coming in since just after we began sitting down. So in all, maybe fifteen or twenty of them were standing around the lunch counter—kind of looking threatening but not saying much—occasionally talking low to each other, and all of us were just sitting there, making like we were studying, although you know we couldn't keep our minds on that.

"Then all at once, the sheriff come in with a couple more of his guys and the head highway patrol, and all the laws commenced to mumble to each other, so I couldn't rightly hear them. But then pretty soon, the high-ups moved up close, and the sheriff said, 'Okay, folks, listen up. Officer Boudreau of the highway patrol and me have our orders to clear out this building and close the lunch counter. And Mr. McCurdy here is the store manager, and he has said he is closing his store for the night. And he has asked me to tell you that if you need to buy something, the store will be open again in the morning at the regular time, but not the lunch counter, so you can get what you need then.'

"We looked at each other—and especially the leaders—to see what we should do. Then the sheriff picked it up again and said, 'So get your stuff together now.' He looks at his watch and says, 'It's eight fifty-five right now, and by nine o'clock, I want everybody but the store employees and our officers to be out of here.' Or words like that."

"Did they do what he said?" I asked.

"Well, not right off," Edward replied. "There's a colored minister, Rev. Kinnard from Natchitoches. He has a PhD and teaches at Northwestern Louisiana State over there, so he's a doctor. But most people know him as a minister. One way or the other, all the young people and most of the coloreds do. Anyway, he acted pretty bold and asked the sheriff by what authority he was making people leave, and what will be the penalty if they don't.

"The sheriff just sort of swelled up when Dr. Kinnard axed that, and sheriff, he fired back, 'What is your name, sir, and where are you from?'"

"Dr. Kinnard didn't bat an eye. He just spoke right up and told the sheriff who he was and where he was from, and like we all knew he would, the sheriff said, 'Well, *Mr.* Kinnard . . .' Like he's damned sure not going to call him doctor. '*Mr.* Kinnard,' he says, 'it looks like you are a long way from home.'

"Dr. Kinnard, he just laughs and says, 'Well, Sheriff, I don't know that I would call seventy-five miles a long way from home. I've heard tell that it's farther than that from top to bottom of Caddo Parish.' Besides half of my students live that far from campus. Some of the sit-ins and some of the watchers in the front door laughed at that, but none of the deputies or patrols did. The deputies commenced to move around and grumble to each other some more and get their clubs out, but little old Mr. McCurdy, the store manager, pipes up pretty loud and says, 'I don't know about that, but I am James McCurdy. I am the manager of this store . . .'

"When he said that, some of the boldest of the sit-ins started applauding. You could tell that sort of got his goat, and when he began to get red in the face, all the sit-ins started clapping louder, and a couple of them whistled. He took a deep breath, and when the noise died down, he went on, saying, 'I have the authority to close this store whenever I choose, and I can tell you now that this store is *officially closed* as of this minute, and anybody that is here without my permission is *trespassing*, and I am hereby requesting Sheriff William Odum here to arrest any and all trespassers immediately.'

"Well you can imagine what a big hullaballoo that caused. Took everybody by surprise. At first we clapped some more and laughed and yelled insults, but then somebody must have called the fire department because we heard their sirens right away, then some more sheriff's cars and patrol cars. And pretty soon, the school buses pulled up and right behind them, and some ambulances.

"A couple of people tried to leave straight out, but young thugs at the entrance hit them with bats and drove 'em back inside. Most of us inside linked our arms and started singing. The sheriff started giving orders, getting his people lined up, and soon as he could, he turned them loose on us.

"They just waded into us with their clubs flying, beating people, throwing them down. I could hear people shouting, one woman screamed. People had blood running down their faces, crying, yelling. There was a bunch of white boys hanging around outside, too, and when they saw it all happening, they ran into the store and commenced to punch and kick and stomp people, right in there alongside the deputies, and the deputies watching and not doing nothin' until the sheriff finally made them stop."

Elvira asked Eddie if people were seriously hurt. He said that he saw two or three people down, and an ambulance driver came in with a stretcher to take at least one to the hospital. "But I didn't know how bad they were injured or where they took everybody," he said.

I asked, "What did y'all and Marlow do?"

"Well," Eddie said, "at first we just tried to stay out of the way. But up front, a lady got knocked down, and it looked like the white kid that hit her was fixin' to hit her again with a stick, and Marlow, he stepped up and jerked that guy's stick out of his hand and kicked him, and the guy fell down, and then a bunch of the guy's buddies piled on Marlow, and we got into it and it turned into a free-for-all for a few minutes. But pretty soon, the deputies started pulling people apart and handcuffing them, And just about the time I thought I was about to get handcuffed, Mr. Lou showed up and he just grabbed each of us by the arm and jerked us out of the pile."

I was surprised to hear Elvira fairly whoop with laughter. She said, "Lord, girl, they say Mr. Lou was a sight to behold. A natural sight to behold! Ain't that true, Edward? They say he stormed into that store like the prophet Ezekiel. And just a few seconds later, he come back out dragging these boys and Marlow by us. The sheriff went to stop him, but Mr. Lou, he just bellered out. I mean *bellered* out. He told the sherriff, 'Goddamn it, Bill,' he said, 'these here's my boys. One's my nephew and three of them is paying customers, and by God, I don't have no customers to spare—or nephews either, far as that goes. You just leave them to me, and I'll keep 'em out of trouble, you hear?' And before the sheriff could say anything, Mr. Lou, he marched the four of them outside and away from the H-E-B parking lot and back down to here.

"Before Marlow done his thing," Elvira continued, "Mr. Lou had just told me to cook these boys some hamburgers and give them a beer." She laughed. "'They couldn't get served worth a damn down at the H-E-B,' he said. And later on, some regular customers come in the café. They weren't too friendly, except some of them that knew Marlow, but they didn't make a scene or anything."

Deciding I had better get what sleep I could, I went back to my room and changed into my dress and my flip-flops. I gathered up my billfold and purse, and put the billfold and my car keys in the purse and pulled a blanket off the bed and lay down on a couch in the office and picked up my book and read for a few minutes before falling asleep.

BACKLASH

In an essential relation . . . the barriers of individual being are in fact breached and a new phenomenon appears . . . : one life open to another . . . attaining its extreme reality from point to point . . . in the depths of one's substance, so that one experiences the mystery of the other's being in the mystery of one's own. [Until] the two participate in one another's lives in very fact, not psychically, but ontically. [11]

—Martin Buber, *Between Man and Man*

I had fallen asleep on the couch in Lou's office. It was about three thirty and not yet daylight when he got back, or at least when he came into his office. I liked waking up and seeing him when he came in.

Groggily, I asked if Marlow was still in jail. Lou shook his head and said, "No. But no thanks to him." He chuckled. "He was sleeping like a baby on one of them hard steel bunks in the cell where they had him. You'd a thought it was a feather bed. Marie Lynn called to him through the bars and told him, 'Marlow, wake up, honey, so we can go home.' Marlow sort of growled and told her, 'Mama, I'm not going home until the others do.' She laughed and said, 'Honey, look around yourself. Do you see anybody else in here but you and me and your Uncle Lou?' He sat up then and looked around a while with big, uncomprehending eyes and said, 'Where'd they go?' She told him they'd all bonded out while he slept. His face turned red. 'I'm the only one left?' he asked like a little boy. I was afraid he was going to cry. Then Marie Lynn whispered, 'Come on, sweetheart. Don't just sit there like an old toad. Your daddy's already posting bond for you up front. Come on. You've done all you can for now, hon. It's time to go home.'"

"So he decided to give up?" I asked.

[11.] New York, Macmillan 1965.

Lou laughed and said, "Yeah. He was still reluctant to leave because Dr. King had suggested people serve their time instead of bonding out in order to slow down the system in the jails and cost them some money, and I expect it hurt that the other protesters hadn't included him in the decision to leave. He told me he didn't know but a few of the people in the sit-in, even though most of them were connected with the college one way or another. He said the coloreds still kind of kept to themselves even with integration and all and with the fear of reprisals for civil disobedience."

My heart went out to Marlow. Such a serious boy, and I couldn't help feeling a little envious of how Lou and his family took up for one another.

Lou said he was going to go grab a couple of hours of sleep, so I picked up my own pillow and blanket and walked a little slowly on back to my room and lay down, feeling anticlimactic and not expecting to fall asleep again. But when I woke up, it was full daylight, and I was inexplicably flooded with happiness.

My watch said it was past nine o'clock. I lay there for a while and—really for the first time since leaving Cindy's—started thinking about what I was going to do next. I wasn't ready to go back to Houston yet. There was too much to be thought through. Also, I had to get some money out of the bank and buy a couple of changes of clothes and figure out what to tell Gerald about the car, and I couldn't just leave my job hanging. I had to do something about that right away with school vacation ending in a couple of weeks. If Gerald and I split up, I'd have to have an income!

Then I began to think about calling Cindy to see if I could figure out a way to begin working on making things right with her if it wasn't too late. It was as if I were Rip Van Winkle, asleep for the last twenty years and just now waking up and beginning to realize that I had missed a lot while life had gone on about its business without me. I couldn't piece together how I could have just sat back and let the love of my daughter evaporate. We had always, I thought, been close when she was little; and somewhere along the way, I had let that slip away. Another gift from the booze, no doubt. At least for the moment, I was more than willing to leave the blame there until I could, as I had so often heard in Daddy's AA meetings, "Get my shit together and get back into my life."

A few minutes into those thoughts, I felt sweat break out on my face; and from under my arms, more sweat began trickling down my sides. I wasn't ready to talk to Gerald yet at all. Too many things had happened, and I didn't know what to say to him. The nighttime visit to the fish tanks drifted back to me. I didn't want to lose what I had found there.

But finally, I stood up and put on what my mother would have called "my poor, old bedraggled dress" again and sucked up my belly and went back over to Lou's office and used his office phone to call the Houston School District.

As it turned out, I got hold of a nice woman in personnel, and she helped me. I told her I was checking to see if there was any way I might take off the fall semester and still keep my job. A few minutes later, she came back on the line and said it looked like I had a lot of vacation days coming and that I might be entitled to a full semester's leave.

She asked if it would be a medical leave, and I said "maybe." She said she didn't see any reason why I couldn't get a medical leave for a semester as long as I had a letter from my doctor, and that would leave my vacation days intact. "But the sooner you let us know, the better, hon," she said. "You know we're always short of math teachers. And it's already the first week of August, and that only gives us a couple of weeks to find a substitute for you." I thanked her and said I would call back as soon as I knew something for sure no later than tomorrow.

Cindy was next. I sat for a while at Lou's desk in the office. It was immaculate. Nothing on it but the telephone, a yellow pad, and a couple of ballpoint pens and a calendar. The books surrounding me were like an old shawl on my shoulders. I sat and read titles and played with one of the pens and resisted getting a book down to read, aware that there were more books in his room and that I hadn't even started on the one I got yesterday. And what was worse, I couldn't even remember yesterday's title. I swore at my hands for shaking for no reason, reflecting that it was demeaning to calibrate my recovery with tremors and lapses of memory and that I needed to find a way to get out in front of myself again. After resting a just a little longer, the aroma of coffee drifted in from Elvira's kitchen across the way.

Dew on the long St. Augustine grass wet my toes and my fancy flip-flops. I smelled oatmeal cooking and toast toasting. When I pushed through the screen door, Elvira looked up and smiled. She surprised me by walking over and giving me a big, long hug and asking how I had slept. Before I could answer, she put her hands on her hips and cocked her head and said, "Is that the only dress you got, girlfriend?"

I'm sure I must have flushed as I nodded. I put together a semblance of a laugh and said, "I always travel light when I'm on the lam."

She laughed out loud and said, "I know that's true, darlin!" She thought for a minute and then said, "You and me about the same size. You may be a little taller. How about I loan you a pair of jeans and one of my nice T-shirts?"

I felt tears spring to my eyes, and I told her that would be wonderful. She took off her apron and said she would be right back. "Coffee's on the stove," she said in what I was coming to think of as her general benediction. As an afterthought, she told me Lou was up already and had told her about Marlow. "By the way," she said, "he wants to talk to you about him moving your car to Marie Lynn's for safekeeping. I think he's probably showering or something now."

I thanked her and fixed myself a mug of their strong Louisiana chicory-fortified coffee milk and told her I would be in Lou's office using the phone. Wading back across the wet grass toward the office, I could feel my heart beating and see my hands shaking as I took care not to spill the coffee. I forced myself to dial Cindy's number. While the phone rang at a disconcertingly slow pace for a very long time, it was hard not to hang up. Then I felt myself go rigid when she finally did answer.

Her familiar voice was full of surprise. "Are you all right?" she said. Then without waiting for an answer, she said, "We've been worried to death about you, Mother. Daddy finally had to go to the police and file a missing person report."

It felt like a cold, damp sheet was squeezing my body head to toes. "That's too bad," I managed finally. "Listen, Cindy, I apologize for the way I left. That's the main reason I am calling."

"But why *did* you, Mother?" she cried. "I was so happy and proud for you and Daddy to see Emily, and I so wanted us to be happy together, and I thought we were. But you acted so strange, and then when I saw you down there with the fish tanks and all . . ." She lapsed briefly into silence then blurted out, "What's *wrong* with you, Mother?"

I took several breaths to steady myself. "As I said, dear, I apologize for leaving and for the way I left. That's why I called." I waited for a response and finally asked if she was still there.

"Yes," she said faintly.

"First of all, I want you to know that I love you, and I think Emily is just darling, and you are so good with her. I don't know where you got that ability. Obviously not from me, but it is very important that you know how proud I am of you—and of Robert too . . ."

"Oh, Mother, this is just so sad. I can't believe you're are even having to *say* all those things—that they even need to be said."

"I know that, Cindy, and I feel the same way. The reason I'm calling is I would like very much for us to figure out how to get together more. I would like very much to visit (I scrambled back from almost saying 'meet with') you in the next couple of weeks and have some time to talk. There is a lot I need to learn from you, especially about your life, and if you are willing, I would like for us to kind of start over on a lot of things with your guidance."

"Where *are* you?" she demanded.

I thought over possible responses, some more humorous than others, and finally replied, "I'm staying with some friends for a while."

"But *where?*"

"In Louisiana."

"In *Louisiana?* Are you in a hospital or something?"

I grinned in spite of myself and pushed back the inappropriate impulses that surged into my mind. Cindy was smarter than she sounded. "No, dear," I said soberly, "just visiting some friends."

"*You* don't have any friends in Louisiana, Mother," she said suspiciously.

"Well, actually I do, Cindy, and probably some relatives too, come to think of it. But let's not go into all that now. I would really like to be able to spend some time with you and Emily and Robert too, if he has time."

"You mean now? Here?"

"Well," I said, treading water, "not right this minute, but in the next few days, and certainly at your place if possible, or wherever."

"How about at home, with you and Daddy?"

"I don't know about that, Cindy. I haven't talked to your father yet."

"He's here. You want to talk to him now?"

"Not quite yet, dear, but soon. Give him my love, and none of you need to worry about me at all. I'm doing fine, and again, I am deeply sorry to have left the way I did, but I thought I had to."

"What do you mean 'you thought you *had* to'?"

I didn't want to follow where the conversation was heading. "Cindy," I said, as cheerfully as possible, "I have to get off the phone now, but I promise to write to you today and try to explain some of those things as best I can. There's a whole lot of old stuff that you couldn't be expected to know about at this point. A lot has happened for me this last year, okay? I love you and am very proud of you."

"I don't understand *you*, Mother!"

"It's nothing deep or sinister, dear. I'll write this afternoon, and you'll see. So take care of yourself and the baby, Cindy, and take care of your father. Give him and Robert my love. I have to go now . . ."

I listened for a while, but she didn't say anything. "Cindy? I'm hanging up now, sweetheart. I love you."

"But I would feel weird giving them your love after all this," she complained.

"Well, I don't want you to feel weird, sweetheart. Don't do anything that you're not comfortable with. If you can though, I would appreciate your letting your dad and Robert—and yourself—know that I care deeply for all of you, and am doing very well now, regardless of how it may seem."

More silence. "Okay, dear, I have to hang up now. Goodbye."

"Bye," Cindy said weakly.

I was shaking so hard that I dived back into my room, got my purse, and rushed back out. Elvira intercepted me the kitchen door. She was holding the promised jeans and several T-shirts. I thanked her and stepped back into my room to change. When I came out again, she asked me if I was leaving. My teeth were on edge with the need not to be seen breaking down; but at the same time, after all her kindness, I couldn't just rush off. Snared by my own impatience, I forced myself to slow down.

I told Elvira the talk with Cindy had been painful, and I needed to go for a short walk to get back on track. I handed her the car keys from my purse and asked her to give them to Lou. She looked at the violent trembling of my hand.

"Hold on just a minute," she said. "I need to tell you something."

I forced myself to stop and looked at her—impatiently, I'm afraid. Her face was strikingly composed and still, and seeing her up close softened me.

"You don't know this," she said, "but since it looks like you and Mr. Lou are getting pretty tight, I'll tell you because you ought to know."

I wasn't so sure I wanted to know whatever it was or that I was ready to accept her assessment of my relationship with Lou, but it looked like I had been elected. I nodded without volunteering more, so Elvira went on.

"Mr. Lou," she said, "was married to a woman named Annie over to Natchitoches, and when they split up, I was pretty young, about the same as Marlow now. I had got into some trouble, and you might say Ms. Annie had took me in and helped me out a lot. She sort of 'took me to raise,' as the saying goes, after she had lost her baby. She gave me what little work she had around her bar so I could earn a little something for myself, but she wanted me away from the bar. Even though she and Mr. Lou had split up, she still kind of watched out for him as best she could without letting him know it. Well, she finally sent me over to him and told me to axe him for a job. He put me to work, and then later on, Ms. Annie told me she would pay me a little extra to look out for Mr. Lou.

"I didn't understand at first. I was just seventeen, and I thought she had something bad in mind that I knew she had saved me from, so I was shocked. But then she laughed and said that wasn't what she had in mind at all but that Mr. Lou had grown up kind of rough and need someone with a level head to watch out for him, 'Keep him from making bad decisions,' she said.

"So over the years, Mr. Lou has got in the habit of talking to me whenever he need advice. He don't know it, but sometimes I don't know what to say, and I get a hold of Ms. Annie and axe her, and she's so smart, she can usually figure out something. Sometimes I suspect Mr. Lou know it's Ms. Annie's advice but would rather just not admit it. Well, yesterday, I seen he was down, and I know he's been worried about you, if you don't mind me saying so. So I axed him what was wrong, and he said the sheriff had him worried. That surprised me because him and Sheriff Odum is pretty good friends.

"So anyway, what he told me was that the sheriff had pulled him off to one side after all the demonstrators had been loaded up and hauled away last night and scolded him pretty bad, saying Mr. Lou had overstep his bounds by interfering with the arrests of our guests and Marlow, and had took advantage of their friendship. Then Sheriff Odum sort of drop a bomb. He said that he had been keeping a eye on you and thought you looked pretty suspicious, and he was afraid you might be a out-of-state organizer for some radical group. Sheriff don't know much about radical groups, but he mentioned SNCC and the Black Panthers and even Dr. King. He said he thought behind that, they all might be tied in with communists, and it was pretty suspicious that you turned up just when our three guests blew in from out of town, and now here you were, staying here and all. And then with Marlow taking part in the sit-in, and everybody know he think highly of Mr. Lou, so Sheriff Odum said he was beginning, as he said, to 'connect some dots,' and he didn't like the picture he was seeing. I guess he was just warning Mr. Lou to stay out of the sheriff's business but also warning him that you and Marlow and probably me might get him in trouble with the law or at least with the Klans."

I couldn't think of anything to say. I wasn't shocked, but I hadn't taken time to look at it that way. The whole business seemed so outlandish that I thought at first she was pulling my leg. Still, I *had* grown up in this country—or close enough to know how dangerous it could be under the surface. I have never seen a lynching, but I sure came of age in an atmosphere that permitted them, and I know that a lot of people outright condoned them—even if for a while, lynching had been uncommon.

Then to be honest, I was a little flattered and even excited, though I wouldn't have admitted it to her because I didn't know her that well yet; but I couldn't remember ever having been taken so seriously. At any rate, I felt flattered, and strangely enough, *comforted* that both she and Lou were concerned about me. And I thought, *Well, whatever.* I'd just walk around outside for a while and get some fresh air for the first time in too long and see if things wouldn't begin to sort themselves out, so I reached into my pockets to make sure I had money and my billfold, and I hit the door.

My stride is naturally pretty long and relaxed looking—so I'm told—no matter what's going on inside me, and I stretched it out when I got to the sidewalk like a race horse on the last lap. Felt like I was almost flying, especially after all the discomfort of the week: the grotesque experience in the café, and the disorientation and misery and loss of control at Cindy's home. The fear, the drinking, the blackouts, and not knowing what all I couldn't remember, but automatically feeling guilty about it—whatever it might have been. Not to mention all those hours alone in the car, mulling over my childhood, the good and bad times with my daddy, and missing him so much like I do most of the time.

A couple of blocks down the road, I saw the drugstore where Elvira and I had sheltered the night before—and a half-block beyond that, the supermarket where the people had staged their sit-in. Remembering that I needed some toothpaste and deodorant and my own brand of shampoo, I walked into the drugstore. It felt marvelous to be out on my own again, even though I was still trying to get clear about my situation and was reviewing my decisions and plans so far—especially my decision to run back to Lou Fontinot's place, even though it still looked like the last place Gerald would ever think to look for me.

I have to admit that I was scared, but it was an anxiety tinged by the excitement of being really on my own and being involved in something bigger than me happening in the world around me, even if it was only on the fringes. Of course, I really didn't get all that dramatic. I had been on my own with Cindy at my parents' home during the war, when Gerald was away in the service and all. But that was different. I mean, that was just being back in my parents' home, not much of an adventure, truth be known; and it felt as if I couldn't move without asking permission or worrying about my mother's disapproval or the troubles she and Daddy seemed always to be having. In contrast with that, now here I was—twenty years older, with very little money, a kind of fugitive, no security, living on the kindness of a man I hardly knew and should have been angry with and maybe afraid of, but with nobody to worry about but myself (bless the Lord). Let me tell you, I'm not exaggerating when I say—for that moment anyway—it was thrilling as all get out!

A man was just opening up the drugstore and was sweeping the sidewalk in front as I came up. He was of medium height and had a wispy kind of little mustache and seemed shy. I smiled at him, but he just stared up at me without smiling. I thought I remembered his face from the crowd around the supermarket last night. I told him good morning, but he still stared without saying anything. For a moment, I thought he might be mentally handicapped; but closer, he looked more surly than incompetent.

I looked at him and thought, *Well, foo on you. I'll just turn you into a Chessie cat.* That was my private in-joke with my dad from my college days. While Cindy and I were still living with my parents, my mother urged me to go back to Stephen F. Austin Teachers College in Nacogdoches—where Gerald and I had gone to school before the war—and take a couple of courses so maybe I would be a little closer to graduating when Gerald got back. Mother had also offered to take care of Cindy herself, or hire somebody to, while I was in class.

I jumped at the chance to go back to school and get out of the house. I had finished two years already with a good record and hoped maybe to get one more year done before Gerald got out of the hospital and came home. It was one of those rare plans that work out like you plan them because as soon as Gerald got his insurance business off the ground a year or so later, I went back and finished my BS with honors in math and got a teacher's certificate, so I knew I was employable.

Anyway, while I was in school, one of my professors told a story about a "thought experiment," involving a cat that was both dead and alive. Well, I remember thinking, *Huh?* and not much else, but I couldn't get the image of that fifty-fifty cat out of my head. It came to me that the cat in the story was like the Cheshire cat in *Alice's Adventures in Wonderland*, always appearing and disappearing, leaving behind nothing but his smile. So eventually, I remembered that my grandmother had a habit of saying so-and-so was "just grinning like a Chessie cat," so Cheshire cat became Chessie cat for me.

Then one day, I told my dad that sometimes *he* reminded me of the Chessie cat because every now and then, I would look at him and it was like I had caught him in the act of disappearing; and after that, I sometimes would call him "Chessie cat" as part of the joke, and he would laugh and make cat noises and claws. But my mother never laughed. She used to put her hands over her ears and yell at us. "Y'all stop that! I can't stand it."

She said it was because she didn't want to hear about any cruelty to animals, but I always thought the fact of the matter was that it cut too close to the truth about her and Daddy, with him always just up and disappearing right before her eyes while she was talking to him. Of course, he didn't really, but that was how it seemed sometimes, and I could imagine it making her skin crawl when we went on like that and her maybe *feeling* the "truth" of it without completely admitting it to herself, and it might have seemed like we were making fun of her. And who knows but what, deep down inside, maybe we were!

Strangely enough, there was something else that came to be connected with the Chessie cat. Once when I was about thirteen, a history teacher scolded me for forgetting to turn in some homework. I was used to being the pet of most of my teachers and couldn't remember ever having been in trouble; so when that happened, being the dramatic child I was, I felt like I would "die of embarrassment."

All of a sudden, I had the startling experience of seeing the teacher, a Mrs. Burke, shoot off into the distance, like I was suddenly peering at her through the wrong end of a telescope. At the same time, her voice seemed to grow tinny and faint and hard to hear. It scared the "pee wadding" out of me, and then it scared me even more when Mrs. Burke stopped talking and stared at me and asked if I was all right. I told her I didn't feel too good, and she had me sit down for a while and put my head down between my knees. I refused to tell her what had happened. From then on though, right up to now, every once in a while, when I get embarrassed or too intensely focused or even just bored, people I happen to be looking at, and sometimes whole scenes, just fly off to the wrong end of the telescope and sort of fade from reality like the

Cheshire cat. It worried me enough that I never told anyone about it until much later after I had met Gerald, and then only him.

Once inside the drugstore, I was pleased that the store had all the things I needed. I liked drugstores and usually would have looked around to see if there was anything else I could think of to get but couldn't now because I was so low on money. But they did have a soda fountain, and I was dying for a cup of coffee or hot cocoa. A man in a deputy sheriff's uniform and a woman wearing the drugstore's staff uniform were sitting at the soda fountain counter chatting and drinking coffee. From a distance, they seemed companionable and relaxed.

When I walked up though, they stopped talking, and the deputy slid off his stool and ambled just a hair too casually back to the back of the store. I chose a stool a couple of places down from the woman, and when the boy—what we used to call the "soda jerk"—behind the counter came over, I ordered coffee and a sweet roll. He said, "Okay," but then he turned and walked away, also back in the same direction the deputy had gone. Ten minutes passed, and my order didn't come. I checked my pocket to be sure I had the money. While I was doing that, I happened to look over at the store clerk just as she stood up and walked away too—but toward the front of the store in her case—and stood there with her arms crossed.

By then, I was remembering what Elvira had told me about Lou's conversation with the sheriff, and I was beginning to feel a little ill at ease. When that registered, the whole scene zoomed away to half normal size. I decided it was time for me to get out of there. I stood up and went over to the store clerk, who was still standing there like a sentry keeping an eye on me, and asked her where I could pay for my shampoo and toothpaste and deodorant. Her name badge said "Millie," so I called her Millie just for effect.

But before she could answer, a gruff voice boomed from behind me. "Can I help you, ma'am?" Startled, I turned to see who had spoken and found myself face to face with the mousey little unsmiling man I had seen at the front of the store when I came in. Deadpan, I asked him where I could pay for my shampoo and things.

"I thought you wanted coffee and a sweet roll," he said accusingly and sarcastically at the same time, leaving me to wonder where he had found out what I had ordered as he no doubt had intended me to.

"Well, I did," I drawled, "but everybody had sort of disappeared, so I decided just to pay up and go find someplace else to get my coffee."

"Who're you waiting for?"

"I beg your pardon?"

"I said, who are you waiting for?" he repeated, loud and mocking.

When I'm irritated, I tend to develop a smart mouth, as I did then. "Well," I said, "that's sort of evolving. For a while, I was waiting for your soda jerk to serve me, then I was waiting for Millie here to tell me where to pay for my purchases, and now I'm waiting for you to get the hell out of my way so I can leave." I shoved the shampoo, toothpaste, and deodorant into his hands and said, "Here's your merchandise back. I won't be needing it."

He put the stuff on a counter and stepped across in front of me so that he was blocking the door. "Lady," he said, "I'm sure your friends back wherever you come from think you're a great comedian, but I want to know who you are waiting for." Out of the corner of my eye, I could see the deputy sheriff edging toward us. I started to step around the man, but when I did, he pushed hard on my shoulder, stopping me in my tracks.

I stood up straight—about as tall as he was—really angry now, and said, "What is your name, mister?"

He said, "That's none of your business."

I could feel myself beginning to boil. "If it's none of my business, mister, then who or what I might be waiting for is none of yours, is it? Now get out of my way."

I started around him again, and he stepped in front of me again. I looked at the deputy and said, "Officer, do you see what this man is doing to me?"

The deputy said, "No, ma'am. I don't see a thing." In an instant, I went from mad to terrified.

The man blocking me said, "All I want to know, lady, is what you did with your niggers." A lifetime in the south sent rivulets of ice down my back. I looked out the front door to gauge my chances of escaping. As I did, another sheriff's car was pulling up. I looked for Millie, who was the only other woman in the store, but she was nowhere to be seen.

I looked back at the car that had pulled up outside and saw Sheriff Odum himself getting out of it. That brought a glimmer of hope. But I realized this might be my last chance and that if the sheriff turned out to be in cahoots with them too, then I was truly in deep, deep trouble. Nevertheless, for the moment, he looked like my only chance.

I turned to the deputy and, with what bravado I could manage, said, "I would like to speak to Sheriff Odum, please."

The deputy's grin vanished. He clearly had not seen the sheriff drive up. Now when he looked toward the front door and saw the sheriff walk in, the deputy suddenly shrank and simultaneously grew animated, singing out to Odum, "This lady says she would like to speak to you, Sheriff."

Odum came up to us with several expressions chasing one another across his face. I put out my hand and introduced myself to him and automatically, he took my hand and shook it, though I could see he had second thoughts about having done so. "What can I do for you?" he asked formally.

"I'm not really sure," I told him. "All that's happened so far is that I have been treated rudely and have not been allowed to leave this drugstore. Just before you arrived, this man (I nodded at the unsmiling man) blocked my path as I was trying to leave and pushed my shoulder hard enough to cause me some discomfort. Then he said he wanted to know what I had done with my 'niggers.'"

The sheriff looked at the man and asked, "Did you say that, Henry?"

"Henry" dropped eye contact with the sheriff and said, "Well, uh, Sheriff, I had to protect my store."

The sheriff looked at the deputy and asked, "Corporal?"

I broke into the questioning before the deputy could answer and told the sheriff that his deputy had been looking directly at me and "Henry" at a distance of about three to five feet from where this was going on but that when I asked him if he had seen the man push me, he had said, "No, ma'am." I told the sheriff that when I heard that obvious lie come out of his deputy's mouth, I had become very frightened.

The sheriff looked at the deputy and said, "Lonnie?"

The deputy turned red and said, "Well, sir. Uh. I guess I didn't know for sure what she was talking about."

The sheriff looked at him sharply, and the deputy turned his eyes to the floor. The sheriff then addressed the man named Henry and said, "Henry, did you push this lady?"

Henry, a little less belligerent now but still fuming, said, "Sheriff, I just restricted her from leaving. I had cause to believe that she was up to no good."

"So what made you think that, Henry?" the sheriff asked conversationally. "Was she shoplifting or something? Hiding merchandise in her purse? Things like that?"

"Uh, not really."

"What then?"

"She was with them people at the H-E-B last night."

"Are you sure? I didn't see her. I didn't see any white women there." The sheriff turned to me and asked, "Ma'am, were you part of that group?"

"No," I said, "But I am acquainted with a couple of the people who were."

"How did you get to know them?"

"They're staying at the motel where I'm staying." I paused to think. "One is the owner's nephew. He works at the motel's café. The other three I ran into yesterday on the back lawn of the motel."

The sheriff turned to Henry and said, "Henry, would you mind introducing yourself to Mrs. Stallings? Henry stepped up, glowered at me, and said, "I'm Henry MacDonald. This is my store, and I can tell you right now that you are not welcome here. Not you or your niggers either." The intensity of his anger almost made me catch my breath.

The sheriff looked from me to MacDonald then asked me, "Mrs. Stallings, would you feel more comfortable discussing this in my car?"

I was still disconcerted that he knew my name, but I didn't want to make an issue of it just then, given that he appeared to be the nearest thing to an ally I had. I nodded and thanked him.

He walked over and opened the front door of the drugstore and then held the passenger-side door of his car for me while I settled into the seat. It was hot in the car, but when he got in, he started the motor and turned on the air conditioner. The car smelled of body odor, but not cigarettes. I dismissed a fleeting fear that he might be planning to take me to jail and, in fact, sat back and welcomed the cooling quiet. I looked at him and raised my eyebrows. "An angry man," I said.

"Yeah," he agreed. "Fear makes a lot of people crazy around here. Henry's not a bad man personally, but you could say he is terrified of change."

I remember thinking, *Well, maybe not profound, but at least thoughtful.* To the sheriff, I said, "I can empathize with that, Sheriff, so long as he doesn't kill anybody."

That statement floated in the air for a while before I asked, "Do you think Henry's in the Klan?"

"I wouldn't be surprised," he said quietly. Then he turned to face me and said, "Not to change the subject too much, Mrs. Stallings, but how much longer do you plan to be in Shreveport?"

At first I thought, this was the start of a "Get out of Dodge speech," but somehow that didn't fit him. For the moment, I was stumped for a satisfactory answer. The truth was that I had no idea how long I would be there, but I also knew that this man could make things hard for me if I sounded sarcastic. Finally, I plunged into a fanciful future. "As a matter of fact, Sheriff . . ." (I wonder how many lies begin with "as a matter of fact.") "That depends on what I find out about my job prospects over here. My mother lives just over the border in Troup, over near Tyler. She's getting along in years, and I've been thinking about moving close enough to keep an eye on her."

The sheriff looked at me, less impressed than I had hoped. "How long have you been thinking about that, Mrs. Stallings?" I felt my shoulders move a little closer to my ears as I wondered if I was really that transparent.

"I beg your pardon?" I asked lamely.

He reached behind the seat and pulled out a clipboard with some papers on it. He leafed through the papers then selected one and detached it from the board and read over it for a few moments. Something about his deliberate movements unnerved me, and I wondered if that was his intent.

"This came to my office this morning, Mrs. Stallings, and I've been wondering what you might know about it."

He held the paper out to me, and I took it, pressing my elbows to my sides to conceal the shaking of my hands and prevent any sweat from running down my sides. "Report of a missing person," it began . . . So Cindy had been giving me a fair warning, whether she knew it or not. "Thirty-eight-year-old white female. Lillian Stallings. Considered to be a possible danger to herself or others. Last seen in a Blue 1959 Pontiac sedan. Gainesville, Florida. August 2, 1960. Believed to be traveling westerly."

"It says here that you have a history of alcohol dependency, that you have been showing what could be signs of early psychosis, and that you have misappropriated a family automobile." He paused to look at me inquisitively as my brain whirled, seeking some kind of effective response. At least I could prove my name was on the car title, along with Gerald's. Finally, the sheriff interrupted my reverie, saying, "Looks like old Henry's not the only one that has it in for you." My body shifted into full terror mode: ringing ears, blazing face, rasping breath. The sheriff didn't say anything. I sat quietly while tears ran down my cheeks. Finally, I agreed with the sheriff that it looked like my husband had pulled out all the stops.

"You must realize that if even part of that is true, I might be asked to hold you until mental health officials can examine you." He paused and looked at me a few moments until his face softened. "What did you do to make *him* so mad?"

I thought about that for a while. When I replied, it was a careful attempt at giving his question due weight. "I can't give you a quick answer for that one, Sheriff. The first thing that comes to mind is to say, 'Just the fact that I left him.' But that's only the most recent step, or final the step, depending on how it turns out. I suspect that the *way* I left him was what hurt because it seemed like a renunciation of what we thought, or at least he has thought, we had in common.

"That includes our daughter and her young motherhood and on and on, and the way it happened made it look premeditated, even though it definitely was not. I overheard my husband and my daughter and her husband discussing turning me over of a mental health professional for evaluation. Whether or not that may have been called for, my career could very well have been in serious jeopardy if they had carried out their plan, so I ran.

"I didn't intend what I did to come out that way, and he may even know that. In a way, the fact that I didn't get mad or hysterical may have made it feel even worse, like calculated or cold blooded."

I paused again, and the sheriff took the opportunity to interject, "Uh, hang on a minute, Mrs. Stallings. It's probably not a good idea to go that deep. Don't tell me what I don't need to know."

My fear was subsiding. Also, I was impressed to hear someone I would usually have expected to have much less depth to be showing some sense and sensitivity. For the moment, I was feeling safe. So I said, "I appreciate that, Sheriff, so tell me what you need to know about me."

"Okay," he said. "my job is to enforce the law and keep the peace in Caddo Parish. These sit-ins may or may not break the law, but they definitely do disturb the peace. I have been told on good authority that they are supported by organizations from outside the parish such as the Student Nonviolent Coordinating Committee, the Black Panthers, maybe the NAACP, maybe the Urban League, and other kinds of agitators. In opposition to those presumed agitators—whether or not they are really involved—are some church groups, the Ku Klux Klan, a whole bevy of politicians, and a lot of ordinary citizens, all getting more and more worked up at each other by the week. And all of that makes it hard for me to do my job."

"And you think I might be working for one of those groups?"

He smiled for the first time and said, "You have to admit, your timing has been impeccable." Thank God we laughed.

I told him, "Okay, Sheriff, I got it. I know it's hard to prove a negative, but here is the truth about me until you tell me to shut up. I admire some of the goals of some of those 'agitators,' as you call them, but I mostly feel uncomfortable in any kind of organization. For the record, I am a card-carrying member of the Houston Teachers Association, the Southern Methodist Church, and the Democratic Party. At the moment, I can't think of any others. I went to college at Stephen F. Austin at a time before students were activists (at least, as far as I knew)."

We chuckled again, and he assured me that he believed me. Finally, as we got serious again, I told him I was glad we had a chance to talk because I needed his help and that I would like to get Lou involved in this talk because there could be ramifications for him as well. The sheriff grew serious and sat up and nodded his head as though to urge me to continue.

"I feel like I'm in both physical and professional danger here. Physical danger because I grew up a hundred miles from here, and I know how the Klan operate. My daddy always said they are doubly dangerous because they're cowards and they feel insignificant, and that makes them mean."

"So what kind of professional danger are you in?"

I pointed to the missing persons' bulletin. "You read what my husband alleged in there. That would make it difficult for anyone who was trying to get a job as a schoolteacher—both crazy and a drunk? Would you hire me to teach your kids? I don't think my husband would give that kind of allegation to a school system because he is smart enough to know he might get sued. And at heart, he's a kind and decent man. But he might do it in anger, or somebody else might get hold of it. The Klan, for example, or a politician, could give it to a newspaper reporter or whatever to discredit the protestors.

"Another thing is that I'm also thinking of taking a semester off from HISD while I look for a job around here."

He raised his eyebrows questioningly.

"Houston Independent School District. I am a math teacher in good standing, and there is a demand for us. I was never a falling-down drunk, and I've never been in treatment or cited for drunk driving. So my official record should be squeaky clean. But now that Gerald has made his allegations public in that bulletin, there is that kind of danger."

"Then you're thinking about staying around Caddo Parish?"

"The idea has its appeal, for now anyway." I told him that now I was just trying it on to see if it fit. But if Gerald and I split, and Cindy was in Gainesville, with my mother not getting any younger in East Texas, and I didn't have anything left holding me in Houston, it could begin to make sense.

"But do you have friends around here?"

"So far, Lou has been a great help, and these are Elvira's clothes. And I've made friends with Lou's nephew Marlow and Marlow's mother, Lou's sister. They live in Natchitoches, and we seem to have a lot in common. She's a librarian at Northwestern Louisiana State."

He cleared his throat. "Yeah, well, I heard about some kind of altercation over at Fontinot's place a week or so ago. You know anything about that?"

I know I must have turned bright red. "Yes, I do, as a matter of fact, and you might say we're still working through that one."

"That's probably another one of those things I don't need to know about."

I smiled, still blushing no doubt. I thanked him for the talk and repeated my hope that he and Lou and I could meet for a consultation. He thought about that for a while and said, "Let me think about the best way to handle that. If you don't mind, I'll need to talk to Mr. Fontinot first, but I'm sure we can work something out."

"Any ideas about what to do about Henry and the Klan?" I asked, hoping I wasn't overstepping.

He said, "I'll probably talk to Henry just to see what he's thinking. That's a hard one to predict. If you don't mind, I would like to keep it quiet for now except for telling Lou about this conversation. I'll be in touch by this afternoon."

Getting out of the sheriff's car, I glanced toward the windows of the drugstore to see if Henry MacDonald was watching. I didn't see him, but I did see Millie the clerk. She waved at me and hurried to the door.

"Oh, Mrs. Stallings," she called out, "could I speak to you for a moment?" I stopped, and she came on out to the sidewalk. "Mr. MacDonald told me to keep an eye out for you and be sure to ring up your purchase when you came out. Surprised, I asked her how much it would be. She said, "If you wouldn't mind stepping inside, I can look at the ticket."

A frisson rippled through me, so I said, "I'm a little confused. This morning, Mr. MacDonald told me I was not welcome to enter the store. Did you know that?"

Flustered, she blurted out, "Mr. MacDonald said you could come in so long as you were by yourself." I couldn't help laughing, and it seemed to confuse her. "Excuse me?" she begged. "Did I say something wrong?" I laughed again and told her to think nothing of it and got my billfold out of my purse and followed as she scurried into the store. Once there, I paid the bill, took my things, and turned to go.

Out of the corner of my eye, I saw MacDonald peering out from behind the pharmacy counter. I waved to him and imprudently shouted to him, "It's safe to come out, Mr. MacDonald. I'm all alone." He didn't answer, and I pushed on out the front door and thought what an idiot I was to provoke a little man needlessly.

Back at the motel, I sought out Elvira in her kitchen. She and Lou were huddled at the long table in the back near the walk-in cooler. Both looked up at me curiously when I came through the door. "How was your talk with Bill Odum?" Lou asked.

"I think it went pretty well," I said. "He seemed to believe me and didn't seem inclined to take me into custody. I guess a lot depends on what my husband does now and what the Klan does. Henry MacDonald was pretty steamed at me when I showed up this morning. He so much as accused me of preparing a sit-in for *his* store and told me not to come back."

"That sounds about right," Lou said. "Something is in motion around here. Elvira got a threatening message today about noon."

I looked at Elvira and asked, "Are you all right?"

"I don't know," she said. "I never been threatened by the Klan before."

I suddenly had a hard time swallowing. "Is this . . ." I asked both of them. "Is this about *my* being here?"

"We were just talking about that," Lou said.

Elvira spoke up. "It may have some something to do with you," she said, "but we figure it's more about the sit-in and those three kids staying here and Marlow." She glanced at Lou, and he nodded. "But they something else you don't know about."

I waited while she thought about what she was going to say.

"You see," she finally began, "I have a partner that live in Natchitoches. I stay mostly here at the motel, but when we get time off or something, I stay with her there in our home, or if she gets somebody to keep her kids, she come here."

"Do the Klan know about you all?" I asked, feeling awkward.

"We keep ourselves as close to invisible as possible," she said. "Our families and a few friends know about us, but they're either supportive or forgiving, depending on how they believe. Not many white people know just because white people generally don't know much about what goes on with black people, but *somebody* know." She handed me a sheet of paper with a typed message that warned in lurid detail what would happen if Elvira and her partner Ada didn't mend their ways or get out of town.

I was suddenly as scared as if the threat had been made to me. "What will you do?" I asked tremulously, imagining the danger faced by these two women who had been so welcoming to me, not to mention the danger faced by the children—Ada's children as Elvira called them.

She grimaced and shook her head. "Right now, we think we'll probably sleep over at Ms. Annie's in Natchitoches. But we both have to work, so we can't just up and leave, at least right away." She looked at me sharply. "This isn't new, and it's not about you. It's where Ada and I live. It's not pretty, but it's home, and Ada, she's got those two children in school."

"So," I barely dared to ask, "will you all take the kids out of school for a while?" The pettiness of my personal concerns compared to hers was piercing. I told Elvira as much. She reached over and patted my hand and said, "Thank you, girlfriend. Trouble's trouble when them folks butt in. We just can't let 'em beat us down no more or turn us against each other. That's what we have to teach Ada's kids."

"What I had in mind." I said, "wasn't just sympathy, but if y'all decide to home school the kids and I'm teaching around here, I might be able to get you books and syllabuses, and maybe do some of the math instruction. Help out until you establish what you're going to do. She grinned and nodded. "Like I said, right now, we probably will stay at Ms. Annie's over in Natchitoches until we see what's going to happen. Looks like things happening all over the south, so the white sheets may not stay interested in us.

"We'll just have to see, but thank you."

I saw her welling up and couldn't keep my composure. It was turning out to be a day of hugs.

Part Four
Joining

If a form and appearance of present being move past me, and I was not really there, then out of the distance, out of its disappearance, comes a second cry, as soft and secret as though it came from myself: "Where were you?"[12]

—Martin Buber, *Between Man and Man*

[12.] Martin Buber, *Between Man and Man* (New York: MacMillan Paperbacks, 1965), 166. (First published 1947, by Routledge and Kegan Paul Ltd. London.)

DOING BUSINESS

If, as Freud suggests in The Ego and the Id, *character is constituted by . . . the ego likening itself to what it once loved—then character is close to caricature, an imitation of an imitation . . . [And] we are making copies of copies, but . . . we have no original, only an infinite succession of likenesses to someone who, to all intents and purposes, does not exist.*[13]

—Adam Phillips, *Terrors and Experts*

If you had told me a week earlier that I would be driving on State Highway 71 from the town of Natchitoches to Shreveport in Louisiana with Lou Fontinot, I would have hooted. If you had told me we would be discussing the finer points of alligator wrestling, I would have thought you were pulling my leg. But there we were, bouncing along the road in his pickup truck like two old buddies. Earlier in the day, I had met his ex-wife, the legendary "Ms. Annie." I had mostly listened as Lou's cook, Elvira, and Elvira's partner, Ada, figured out a schedule for the two of them and Ada's children to take refuge over the coming weekend and beyond until they could figure out what the local Ku Klux Klan were likely to do in retaliation for a sit-in that had occurred at the H-E-B supermarket in Shreveport. If you didn't know they were talking about avoidance of pathological people with sinister intent, you would have thought they were planning a church picnic.

Elvira said Ada had grown up in Natchitoches, so Ada and her kids would likely be safest there with relatives. Elvira said that—being both black and lesbian—they were used to death threats, insults, and crude intimidation. Earlier, I hadn't been able to keep from asking why they didn't move to another city. They looked at each other and smiled. "I guess we prefer the devil we know," Ada said. Elvira nodded. "And the Klans think we are 'armed

---

[13.] (Cambridge, Mass: Harvard University Press, 1995), 77.

and dangerous.'" They both burst into laughter. "And that's the truth!" Ada continued, laughing. "I'm here to tell you, Elvira with a shotgun is just pure old death walking—just ask the chickens."

"You shut your mouth," Elvira said.

Talking over her, Ada said, "Tell Lillian about your great cotton mouth hunt."

Elvira mock glowered while I begged them to tell me, and Ada finally obliged, still laughing the whole time. Elvira, Ada said, was spending the night in Natchitoches one time, when around one in the morning, "We had just turned off the TV and were fixing to go to bed when a big ruckus broke out among the chickens that stay under the house.

"I thought it was cats or raccoons or something after the chickens, you know? Well, so we keep an old shotgun of my daddy's behind the kitchen door and *made the mistake*," she emphasized, cutting her eyes around at Elvira, "of telling Vira to hand me the shotgun from out in the kitchen."

"But instead of doing what I told her, Elvira took it in her head to *keep* the gun and go out and see for her own self what was going on. Next thing I knew, she had grabbed up a flashlight and ran out the back door.

"Then almost immediately, she commenced to yelling, 'It's a snake! It's a snake!'"

"I yelled back at her to give me the gun and ran to the back door, but Vira was already in the yard, chasing the chickens, which were chasing the snake," Ada said. "The moon was bright as daylight when I looked out the window, and with that and the flashlight, I could see these two old hens was chasin' that big old water moccasin across the yard, pecking his tail for all they were worth." She laughed loudly.

"That in itself was hilarious," she continued, "but then suddenly, *Blam! Blam!* Both barrels of the old shotgun went off with huge flashes of fire and lit things up like high noon. I saw Elvira topple over onto her back. That scared me because it looked like she had hurt herself, and I ran out the back door after her, but then I looked again and saw both chickens down in the dirt, kicking their last! And that old cotton mouth just disappearing off into the weeds, and Vira was standing up and rubbing her shoulder."

Lou had come in on the end of the story. He nodded and grinned at what was obviously a familiar tale, but then he changed the subject, suggesting that it might be a good idea for him to follow Elvira's car to and from Natchitoches for a week or two until things cleared up. Nobody was enthusiastic about that, but finally, Lou said, "Well, let's plan on that until a better idea comes along."

Elvira said, "Sure, let's see."

I was inspired to offer, "I guess maybe you could let Elvira ride shotgun," and most of the adults who heard me were generous enough to laugh.

The rough and tumble fun Lou had been having with his two generations of nephews and nieces had felt like something that happened often. His brother Claude, twelve years older than Lou, was a somber-looking farmer; the only one dressed in bib overalls, which he wore on Sunday, with a white dress shirt and shined black dress shoes. Claude's grown children and their kids were there, as were the children of the morose older sister Jeanine, serious and stolid as Claude. Jeanine's brood, like Claude's, included grandchildren—although I got the impression that she was a widow.

Marie Lynn was there. I had already met her the night of the now-infamous sit-in. She was with her husband Kyle. Of course I had seen their son Marlow every day at the café. Once they got over my being there, Lou and Marlow had relaxed into an easy intimacy that was similar to the way Lou and Marie Lynn treated each other. For that matter, Marie Lynn had opened to me immediately. She twinkled and smiled a lot, and we had barely met when she began kidding me about "making eyes" at her big brother. I felt my normal reserve evaporate in her company and looked forward to knowing her better.

After meeting all the friends and relatives and in-laws who had dropped in to see Lou (and, I suspected, to satisfy their curiosity about me), I was curious about what secrets might lie under all those layers. I joked to myself that I was "just downright smitten" with the whole bunch.

I noticed that when I was in the café, I wanted to know more about the photographs of Lou and other people posing with alligators and snakes. Normally, I would have turned up my nose and curled my upper lip. "Mindless machismo and heedless animal cruelty," I mumbled like a mantra until it turned to pure self-mockery. When I had mentioned to Lou before that I was curious about alligator wrestling, he had made a joke of it, saying he thought all women were drawn to Tarzan.

"Yeah?" I scoffed. "Well, you're not exactly Johnny Weissmuller, and I'm damned sure not Jane."

His response was to grin crookedly and say, "But I could be his daddy."

Now on the road back to Shreveport at a little before noon, it seemed like a natural time to find out about how his nephews supplied reptiles for his shows—how they caught them and transported them, and from that we segued, into more about the alligator wrestling itself.

"So when you grapple a poor old alligator into submission," I said finally with fading mockery. "How do you feel? Triumphant or what?"

"More like relieved, really." He pondered that, spreading out his hands on the steering wheel. "I feel different things at different times. Sometimes full of myself. Sometimes relief. Sometimes just that I need a shower. Always glad it's over."

I asked him, "What makes you glad to have it over?"

He laughed. "Well, what do you think? Here's a grown man. He dopes up these really primitive big old animals. Pens them up so they can't get away. Singles out one and does a few tricks with him that make the old gator start out looking mean, and then in the end, subdued by the brave, masterful human."

"You mean it feels like you have insulted the animal?"

"No. No. Not at all." He laughed. "Can you imagine an alligator feeling insulted? The alligator's just a prop I use to act out this fantasy. If I think about it, I tend to feel foolish."

"But isn't it dangerous? Why do you still have all your fingers and toes? Aren't the alligators dangerous?" I asked, maybe rhetorically.

"Sure," he said, "in a way. I guess it might eat me if it was hungry. They don't get hungry as often as a mammal that size. And that's a good thing." He turned to grin at me. "But even if it was starving, its chance of having me for lunch would be pretty slim if I pay attention. The show we put on is designed to create the illusion that the gator thinks like a human. It's dangerous in the sense that a rock rolling down a mountain is dangerous."

"So you think of alligators as being, sort of, just forces of nature?"

"Yeah, I guess so, something like that. Something big and heavy and powerful and fast. But not dangerous like you or me or John Dillinger, not evil or cunning."

"So what does the struggle itself feel like? And I'd like to come back to where I started: how do you feel like afterward?"

He put me off with some jokes but finally took my questions seriously.

"Well, I guess I don't feel skillful or graceful. It's not like a bullfight with swords and ballet slippers and tight pants and all like that. Nobody thinks of alligators as being particularly brave like some people do bulls. Alligators are too ancient for that, and uncomplicated." I asked what he meant by that. He paused then and finally said, "I guess I think of an alligator as a kind of rough draft of an animal. The cliché in the gator wrestling business is that you've got to 'respect' them, but I don't respect 'em. I don't see much to respect, but I *am* afraid of 'em, to be honest." He grinned. "But then I get scared pretty easy."

"When I was a kid working for the carnival, I was sort of drafted into being the carnival boxer, taking on whatever rube wanted to fight. I hated that. I don't think I ever had a prize fight where I wasn't just about scared to death."

"Why were you drafted into prize fighting?" I asked.

"I don't know," he said. "At fifteen, I was already as big as I am now." He seemed to reminisce for a moment. "And the sister of the real prize fighter . . . she was the belly dancer. She wanted her brother to stop because he was getting too old and slow. I guess she talked me into it."

I asked him why he didn't quit when he found out what it was like.

"I think I was more afraid of making the other carnival people mad at me. They were sort of like a family."

"The worst thing about it may have been that there was no way to win. If the guy was a bum, I felt sorry for him. If he was a good fighter, he scared me."

He frowned and moved his jaw around. "This is going to sound dumb, but sometimes I think I sort of identify with the alligators." He looked over at me and grinned self-consciously. "But I try not to let them know that." We commented back and forth, building jokes onto what he had said until we both fell into a slightly uncomfortable silence.

"But you know, going back to your question, I'm always fascinated by how they feel," he said finally.

"The alligators?"

He paused. "Yeah," he said finally. "The thing is, they're mostly just a few big long muscles, and when they work 'em, they're strong as all get out—like a wave in the ocean you float along on all smooth while you're on top, but then when it breaks over you, it's like being pushed by a freight train, and I told you before about their skin."

"Yes, I remember, you told me, 'Soft as a puppy's nose.'"

"Yeah," he said enthusiastically. "You can get caught in the undertow between them two pictures of the animal. You know? Or you can get kind of crazy and convince yourself the alligator could be friendly."

"But the weirdest thing of all is that sometimes I would finish a show and suddenly realize that I was horny! Now is that crazy, or is it just plain sick? Trust me, I have no unnatural desires about alligators, but there you are. So maybe it is the risk or the just plain weirdness of wrestling a creature like that."

As well as I thought I had already come to know him, it still startled me to hear such a big, shambling, scar-faced old man pick his way through sentiments like that. Without realizing it, I reached out and touched his shoulder, I guess wanting to feel closer to him. My gesture took him by surprise, and he jerked his head around abruptly with wide eyes—only to smile shyly and turn back to the road.

Of course, what came up for me were my son-in-law Robert's fish and my daughter's response when she had seen me pressing up against that column of fish tanks. I tried to describe the incident to Lou without making myself sound like a completely deranged slut. But suddenly, I very much wanted him to know what it felt like when the boundary between me and the swimming fish just vanished so that I was entering the fish, and they were swimming into and through me in turn. "It was like my eyes were no longer actively seeing but were simply being open, like when you leave doors open to the night air—except in this case, half-visible shapes could come and go without disharmony." The entire experience pervaded me.

"I just took a deep breath and opened myself up and found this curious fish hanging there before me, and I could feel him as though he were swimming into my eyes and I was swimming into his, and I just pressed myself up against the glass, and I thought I could sense through my belly a hundred tiny impacts of fish bumping against the glass."

Lou had slowed the car and was looking at me intently. I hurried to go on before I lost my nerve, and I practically *confessed* to him, "And it was like I suddenly could *understand* death of all things, and at the same time, tremble under the overblown fear of it." Having said that, I sank back against the seat and felt my shoulders soften and all the rest of my muscles go limp and warm.

"So what happened then?" he asked, deeply engaged.

I laughed. "Believe it or not, at that moment, Cindy turned on the light and saw me, and it scared hell out of her. She said, "Oh, Mother, you're not drinking again are you?'"

Lou groaned.

"No, but then she said the dearest thing, something I still cling to when I think about our problems. She asked me, 'Do you like my baby? Do you know, Mother, I imagine sometimes when I am with Emily that I am you and she is me.'"

Lou and I both were silent for a while, and then he said, "No wonder it upsets you so much to think she is mad at you."

Suddenly, he laughed; and for a moment, it hurt my feelings, but he explained, "Sorry. It finally come to me to think that at last this beautiful woman gives me the time of day at my age—and wouldn't you know, she would turn out to be hot for fish." I looked at him and saw that he was blushing.

But before I could comment, he pulled over onto an intersecting road. "This is Coushatta," he said. "This is the seat of Red River Parish. When Bill Odum contacted the sheriff of Red River Parish to see if he had heard anything about Ku Klux Klan activities after the sit-in, this is where most of the planning seemed to focus."

I asked if that meant they know that Elvira and Ada have connections in Natchitoches and have to travel through here to get there and back and forth to Shreveport.

"Yeah, and the Coushatta Massacre happened here, right at the beginning of the end of Reconstruction."

"You don't mean to say the KKK started here?" I said.

"No, not at all, but this was one of the first places for that kind of overt terrorism—here and a lot of places, and the Klan would like to take credit for it. You probably know the stories as well as I do."

"Probably," I agreed. Actually, my personal connection went farther than that—to great-grandfathers and Lord knows how many great-uncles and cousins, who had been among the good-old-boys. I had grown up with more than enough of their bombast and swagger. Fortunately, in my generation, it seemed to be dying down to a kind of class marker.

"Yeah," I told Lou, "I grew up on stories of the White Citizens' Council and all that. It's too bad really that it leaves such a bad taste in my mouth. I'm sure if I don't settle in Texas near my mother (scary thought), I will want to find a place somewhere on the Red River, but right now, I'm mostly concerned about what part of that meanness has trickled down to here and now."

We got back to Shreveport about two thirty in the afternoon. Lou surprised me by saying that he was glad we had made it back before the drugstore closed. "I want to talk to Henry, and I want him to associate you with me, like he already associates Elvira," he said. I wasn't quite sure what to think about that.

"But Elvira works for you," I said. "Of course you have a responsibility for her safety." It occurred to me that he was getting a little too much involved in taking care of everybody, but I didn't quite know how to challenge him. I suddenly felt like the vulnerable lone female straying too far from the herd with predators around. Something about that feeling I couldn't shake off.

As we reached the drugstore, I told Lou to drive around the block. He looked at me quizzically but passed the store and turned right at the next cross street. The street was empty, and I asked him to pull over to the curb. He switched off the motor and turned to face me. "Okay," I said, "I need a couple of minutes to sort this out. He turned back and sat, staring through the windshield. It took several starts, but finally I told him as gently as I could that although I appreciated his taking up for me, it was beginning to feel demeaning. Finally, I got around to asking him not to get into an argument with MacDonald over the pushing incident. At first I thought his feelings were hurt—and they may have been—but finally, he said, "Okay, but I think it's a mistake just to let it go."

I was relieved and appreciative and told him so. I also told him I would like to talk about it some more when we had more time, when maybe he could help me figure out what I wanted to do.

In spite of all that, as we walked up the sidewalk to the drugstore, I was just two degrees short of terrified. Lou asked me if I wanted to do the talking. I told him that I really didn't but that I didn't want to just sit there like a dummy either. He said he would follow my lead but that mostly he had a proposal that might bring MacDonald into "the club," as he put it. I didn't know what he meant, but I really wanted to kiss him then. Instead, being me, I made a joke. I said as lightly as possible that if he suddenly noticed that I had walked out of the meeting, it would just be to throw up, and he shouldn't worry about it because I would be right back.

As we entered the store, I noticed Millie the clerk and wondered humorously if she ever got to go home. She looked at us nervously until Lou said, "Hi, Millie. Is Mr. MacDonald here? She nodded and said, "Yes, sir." She looked at me as though I had just escaped from the circus.

"Could you let him know Mrs. Stallings and I would like to talk to him if he has time?"

"Uh, sure," she said and walked quickly toward the back of the store. This time, I noticed that there was a counter back there with a sign over it that said, "Customer Service." The irony did not escape me. Millie went through a door in the back wall. She had been gone only a short time when the door opened again, and Henry MacDonald came out, leaving Millie stranded in the doorway.

"Hi, Lou," MacDonald said tentatively.

"Hello, Henry," Lou replied formally. He nodded his head in my direction. "I believe the two of you know each other."

MacDonald said just as formally, "Hello, Mrs. Stallings."

I drew myself up tall as possible and nodded and said in what I hoped sounded like a neutral response, "Hello, Mr. MacDonald," trying not to feel like a kid bringing in her big brother to scare a bully. It worried me that I might have come across as too deferential.

We stood in tableau for several heart beats then Lou broke the silence. "I was wondering if we could maybe find a place to sit down and talk a little," he said. "I have an idea that I think you may find interesting.

First, Henry looked toward the lunch counter, and then he changed his mind. I suppressed a smile, wondering what kind of replay of my last visit might be playing in his head. Finally, he said, "Come on back to my office. Would you all like something to drink?" We both shook our heads, and he led us back toward the "Customer Service" area.

Once inside the small office, Lou came right to the point. "I understand from Sheriff Odum and Mrs. Stallings that there was an altercation here at the store yesterday, but I'm not here to talk about that."

However, MacDonald seemed intent on talking about it, and he said tightly, "She was loitering."

"So you told her, 'Madam, I can't have you loitering here, so I'll have to ask you to leave.' Something like that?"

Henry flushed. "Well, pretty much."

"Just for the hell of it, Henry," Lou said with a smile, "I've heard the word loitering all my life, but I'll be damned if I know exactly what it means. Could you help me out with that?"

MacDonald said, "Well, sure. It means hanging around where you have no business being."

Lou looked confused, "So when you have customers shopping, how can you tell the customers from the . . . what do you call them, loiterers?"

MacDonald was blushing, "Well the thing is, Lou, a loiterer is somebody who just hangs around, and a customer is somebody who is shopping."

"Now I'm really confused," Lou said. "I thought Ms. Stallings was at the checkout, waiting to pay Millie for some things she wanted to buy."

I laughed without mirth. Lou looked at me with raised eyebrows and said, "I'm sorry, Ms. Stallings, I know you didn't want to rehash that altercation now, and here I go like a big dog just jumping right into the middle of it. Would rather put that off? Because I have some other stuff to talk about now. I just didn't want Mr. MacDonald to think we were avoiding the issue."

I looked at MacDonald appraisingly until he began to fidget and clear his throat. Then I said, "Well, Mr. Fontinot, Mr. MacDonald and I have some things to discuss, but at this point, I think they are between him and me. I think, this afternoon, I would rather hear what you have to say."

Lou looked at MacDonald and asked if that was all right with him. MacDonald nodded and cleared his throat and said in a breaking voice, "Lou, this is God's truth. I was trying to protect this woman. I seen her with those colored people at that so-called sit-in at the H-E-B, and I know there are some real hotheads around here that are more than willing to take the law into their own hands and cause her a world of hurt."

Here his voice took on a wheedling tone as he said, "And you too for that matter, Lou, for harboring her and those three white radicals that was staying at your place and that nigger cook of yours. All them together could make things look pretty bad for you. I hear the cook even has a nigger girlfriend out of town, and Shreveport is a Christian city. I know there are plenty of good Christian people ready to put a stop to that kind of blatant sinfulness too . . ."

Lou interrupted him saying, "Henry, I appreciate your concern for Mrs. Stallings's safety and mine, and the safety of my motel guests and employees and all, even if you don't approve of their politics or apparently the race of the black ones. I swear, you sound pretty knowledgeable about that stuff. You know, come to think of it, I might be smart to consult you for suggestions on our security over at the café. Maybe you and I need to talk about that some time." He raised his eyebrows and nodded his head. "If you're willing," he added.

MacDonald muttered something that sounded like, "Well, sure."

"Great," Lou said, "but right now, I have something else to propose that I think stands a chance of reducing that level of anger and suspicion you speak of. So I wonder, would you be interested in hearing my proposal?"

"Okay," MacDonald said with a palpable lack of enthusiasm.

"Okay!" Lou said, "I guess we are enough in agreement to work together. So here's what I propose: I would like to contact some of the other business owners from this side of town and have everybody come to my place for breakfast next Monday morning before we open up, and maybe regularly. First breakfast is on me. No alligator meat. Promise. Okay?" Lou laughed. "Do you like alligator meat, Henry?"

"I never tried it," Henry said, smiling for the first time.

"Well, if you tried it, you might like it. It's kinda like frog legs. Let me know, and I'll be glad to fry you up some sometime, but not Monday. Okay?"

Henry nodded, still smiling. "Nothing but coffee and grits and eggs and bacon and my own special sausage. How's that sound?" MacDonald still smiled and nodded. "And Elvira's biscuits. You ever try any of her biscuits, Henry?"

"Can't say as I have," Henry said, still smiling.

"Well, you come on in Monday and try 'em, and I guarantee you won't ever want nobody else's biscuits. Okay?"

"I'll be there," Henry said.

"Good." Lou responded. "And we can all get together and talk about how we're going to cope with the changes that's happening in this country, but 'specially here in Shreveport. So if the need should come up for joint action, we can figure out a way to coordinate it and stay out of the newspapers and off television and all that."

Lou looked out the window. "This Monday, we probably won't get many people, maybe just some folks from around here like you and me, and probably McCurdy from over at the H-E-B and a few other business owners we happen to know. I know a few. I figure if we get ten or fifteen next week on short notice, and people think it's a good idea, it can grow. Probably mostly people in retail and services like you and me. Bring anybody you want, okay? No matter what race, religion, or political party. Even Cajuns. Right, Henry?"

"Well, I don't know . . ." MacDonald began.

"You going to rule out Cajuns, Henry?"

MacDonald grinned and said, "Naw, Lou. You know what I mean."

"Listen here, son . . ."

Lou's voice dropped and softened, and I thought, *Son? MacDonald's my age if he's a day!* I looked more closely at Lou. He had leaned in close to MacDonald. I expected him to put a hand on the younger man's shoulder at any moment as I watched "Uncle Lou" emerge like a new presence in the room. And I thought, *My god, he's smooth!*

"How're we going to reach agreements that keep the peace just preaching to our own choir? If only one side's in the club?" Lou asked, switching to the inclusive "we." "Besides, don't you want as many customers as you can find? I sure as hell do. So what d'you say we open the door as wide as we can, and once we get a bunch of people in here, let's see what kind of club *they* want."

"I guess we could try that," MacDonald said hesitantly, "but some of 'em aren't going to like it if you let colored in."

"You never can tell," Lou said, that gap in his eyebrow twitching as he broke into a grin. "They say all money's green, yeah? I know you've heard that old saying," Lou said. "Anyway, we're bound to get some that don't agree with us and some we don't even like. Personally, I'd like to keep out the politicians, but this is important, Henry, we don't want to violate our own principle of inclusion. I know you believe that."

Now Lou nodded his head, and I watched in amazement as MacDonald matched him nod for nod. "It was up to me, I think we need to admit anybody who behaves himself or herself." Lou laughed conspiratorially. "But I'll admit I wouldn't begin to know how to enforce that. Can you imagine having politicians in the group and trying to keep them from kissing babies and picking pockets?"

Finally, I had had about all I could take of this "Old Boy schmooze" session. Breaking my long silence, I asked, "What about the Klan?"

Lou glanced at me, and then he and I both looked at MacDonald. He was so deep into the trance Lou had woven that he was truly startled. "What?" he said. "Why are you looking at me?"

Lou said, "I don't know, Henry. I think somebody told me you were on okay terms with the Klan."

For an excruciatingly long time, the three of us just stared at one another, until finally, I was getting fed up as well as embarrassed, so I came flat out and said, "Are you a member of the Ku Klux Klan, Mr. MacDonald?" He looked at me with bug eyes, and he swallowed, and I watched his Adam's apple bob up and down a time or two—apparently blocking speech. Finally, I decided if I was in for an inch I might as well go in for a mile, so I just bored on in. "Well," I said, "are you?"

"Wait a minute," Lou said to me. "I'm not so sure I want to know the answer to that question." He checked MacDonald visually then continued. "But anyway, we've already agreed to accept anybody who behaves." Lou stared off to one side for a few seconds. "Anyway, the Klan is a kind of political party," he added, aiming an inclusive chuckle at MacDonald then turning to throw me a covert wink.

I was mollified. I laughed and said, "Okay," but that I'd feel out of place if I were an East Shreveport businesswoman and a bunch of guys turned up wearing hoods.

We got through that one somehow. I hardly remember how, come to think of it. Lou and MacDonald talked on for a while about how to keep in touch or something bland. I was pretty drained from the day, and it looked like the conflict had been averted; and to be honest, I was on the verge of falling asleep when suddenly, Lou dropped a quiet little bomb.

"Just one more thing," he said as we were standing up to leave. "Whoever comes to breakfast, I am always responsible for the wellbeing of my motel guests and café customers—and my employees—and I know I laugh and joke a lot, but, Henry, I want you and me to make sure that everybody we invite understands that I take that responsibility very seriously."

There it was, just lying out there on the floor like something the cat dragged in, smelling to high heaven; and clearly, neither MacDonald nor I was willing to pick it up, so what we did was just pretend it wasn't there. Shortly after pregnant pause, we shook hands all around and acted as friendly as car salesmen; but there was no gaiety, and I was not practiced enough at this kind of "Old Boy bullshit" to feel at all comfortable with it.

Lou got into his truck, but I went over to his window and leaned in for a light kiss and told him I wanted to walk back to his place to shake off the stress. Marlow's pickup was in the parking lot. He and Elvira had driven back from Natchitoches and were running the café. I was relieved not to have to do that. A couple of other cars were in the parking lot—early diners no doubt.

I rounded the parking lot and made my way down the walkway to the back of the building and stuck my head in at the back screen door to let them know we were back, but Lou was already there, so I just waved when Elvira looked up and headed on over to the office to wait for Lou. As long as no guest came to the office, we would have it to ourselves.

Lou came in a little after that. I was learning that while it wasn't hard to read him when he wanted to be read, he tended to remain hidden otherwise. He came through the door and silently checked for a light on the answering machine and glanced over the guest register. "What do you think?" he asked, joining me on the couch and slouching back to the other end of it. I kicked off my new loafers and put my feet up on the couch, just touching his leg.

I took a deep breath. "Lou," I said reluctantly, "before we go to work on a postmortem, of that round with MacDonald, I need to do some housekeeping talk with you."

His eyes opened in surprise. "Are you putting the brakes on?" he asked.

I was surprised by the uncharacteristically anxious overtone in his question. "Is that how I sounded?" I asked.

He nodded, and I said, "I'm sorry." I leaned forward and squeezed this thigh. "There's just a couple of things I need to clear out of my head before they get lost in strategizing."

He nodded.

"Okay," I began. "First of all, I want to thank you for all your help."

He nodded again. Cautiously, he started to speak again then closed his mouth and waited.

"I don't know what I would have done without it," I said quietly. "But now, I would like to ask an even bigger favor. I would like to stay here for a while longer. Maybe quite a while, but right now, it is important to me to begin paying my way." I laughed on purpose. "Don't want folks thinking I'm a kept woman."

Again he nodded, still more serious than the tone I was shooting for.

"For the time being, I would like to pay regular rent for my room here for a few weeks and add something for board and storage of my car. Okay?"

He nodded again thoughtfully, maybe just beginning to relax.

"Next, I would like to ask you to drive me to Marie Lynn's house early in the morning, so I can get my car. I need to go to Houston to pick up some clothes and a few other things and to get some money to operate on. That will mean staying overnight, so I can go to the bank Monday morning and then maybe stop back by my mother's on the way back here—just to let her know something of what I am up to.

"I have to be back Monday night though because I have an appointment Tuesday with the personnel department of the school board. I called them yesterday and got an appointment, and the woman I talked to said that there are some job openings for math teachers that I could fill on an emergency Louisiana teaching certificate until I can get a regular certificate, depending on what they would be willing to pay me.

"It probably will take all day Tuesday to get the paperwork done for that, and to expedite that, I may even be forced to drive over to Steven F. Austin to pick up a transcript if they need it right away. I've already ordered one by phone, but I don't know how long it will take to get here. I would like to begin work by the end of this month.

"If everything falls into place, I would like eventually to get a little house or apartment or something here in Shreveport.

"What a goofy statement that is, 'if everything falls into place.' Like a puzzle solving itself. But that's down the road. Another crazy sentence: what the hell is down the road?

"And anything you're against me doing when it comes to people around here and all, I won't do it. I mean, I need you to guide me so I don't step in anything and fuck it up out of ignorance. I'm smart, but I'm short on information.

"Meanwhile, Gerald and I have to get started through the process of divorce and division of assets and all that horror . . . And I have promised myself to rebuild my relationship with Cindy and start getting to know my granddaughter. What a hoot that is! I don't even know what that means, let alone how I might be able to pull it off. I have also been pretty neglectful of my mother lately and would like to see what can be done about mending that while she's still alive and I still have time."

I sensed a movement on the other end of the couch. Lou had scooted down to my end and was holding both of my hands lightly in his big, scarred paws and looking intently at my face. I found that I was crying. Not sobbing, but just quietly leaking tears. I looked up at him and smiled, and he said "What would you like for me to do right now?"

I thought hard for a few seconds, and then replied, "Hold me, I guess. I seem to be coming apart."

He moved all the way up to my end of the couch and put his arms around me, and leaned back and didn't say anything for a long time.

"The big reason I want to move here, Lou, is to be close to you and your family and friends because you appear to have something I can't quite put my finger on but feel like I need desperately. No doubt you have figured out that I don't know much about making friends and giving love. I am feeling so happy right now that I'm scared it might just be a pink cloud as we say in AA. I wouldn't want to swear by these emotions yet, and don't want to make big decisions prematurely, especially coming down from a binge like the one I pulled last week.

"And of course, I haven't asked you about any of this, so just stop me whenever you need to.

"I realize I'm babbling, Louis, but there's some sense in there somewhere. I know I am partly responsible for stirring up this hornet's nest of reaction from the Klan and all, even if I'm not in the center of it. I want to help, not just be a spectator, and I want to join you all if you will let me and if it won't cause you harm."

Lou looked at me for a long time, and then finally, he said, "We don't have to do anything right now. We could take a nap or go get some food or something. Let's just sit here for a while like this and see what happens." I closed my eyes and stopped crying, and pretty soon, I fell asleep. When I woke up, he was still holding me and was snoring lightly. My left leg had gone to sleep, and it was bothering me. When I began wiggling my leg, he woke up and asked me how it was going. It was beginning to turn dark outside.

He asked me how I was feeling, and I said, "Much better."

"Okay. Let's get to work on our meeting with MacDonald and see what we can puzzle out for a next move. We've still got some time tonight and the drive over to Natchitoches in the morning. By the way, you might want to get Marlow to drive you in to Houston in his truck, so he can help you load stuff."

Interesting that I was so unused to asking for help that it had not occurred to me to ask Marlow or anybody else to help me. And immediately, I quailed, trying to imagine what I might talk about with Marlow on that long drive. I swallowed that down and held it for later. I nodded to Lou to keep from having to answer.

"So meanwhile, what did you make of Henry?" he said, and I thought, *Oh my god, it's starting.*

I looked at him carefully and took a deep breath and said, "First, would you kiss me?" He did, and when we got through with that, I told him, "I have no idea how to assess his reaction. I was really impressed with your proposal and the way you handled him and all. I'm just naturally skeptical of anything reasonable working with him."

He nodded and said he had some of the same misgivings, but that he couldn't help liking him in a way.

I agreed and pointed out that when Lou had been kind to him and called him "son," it looked like he was ready to be adopted. "And," I added, "I can't thank you enough for going all the way in warning him off of me and Elvira. Naturally, he's afraid of you. You're everything he isn't. At one point, I watched him soften, and it softened me too, and I thought, 'Well, bless his little heart, he just wants a daddy.' But then his eyes changed, and I thought, deep down inside, how lost and terrified—and *dangerous*—he is."

Lou nodded. "He is all of that."

"Of course, I'm biased because he scared hell out me once, and that time he had me in his power in the drugstore, I think he was capable of any kind of meanness. So to be honest, I'm sure not willing to bet my life or yours or Elvira's on his having a change of heart and keeping his word or even being able to do that if he wanted to. I told you what my daddy always said about those cowardly little Klan guys, and fairly or not, that's the basket I still put Henry him in."

I thought a little longer and added, "Since you ask, I'm mostly worried for you. I'm afraid that after he realizes how much he capitulated to you, he could just as easily freeze with hatred."

As I spoke, I felt tears in my eyes again and my throat closing. Without thinking, I reached out and touched his shoulder again. This time, Lou scooted down the couch and pulled me in close and held me again as I sort of collapsed onto his chest, and as soon as I felt the surge of safety that came with that, I just opened the spigot and let all the fear pour out of my eyes and nose.

Normally, I couldn't stand to be held—hated the feeling of helplessness that went with it—but I held on without speaking or squeezing my eyes or indicating in any way that I should stop crying. Lou just held me tight while I blubbered snot all down the front of his shirt.

After I wound down and blew my nose on God knows how many Kleenex till I thought it would fall off, I sat back, and Lou sat back and looked at me and smiled and said, "You hungry?"

"Ravenous," I said.

"There's a IHOP out on the highway. Think we could find something out there?"

And I said, "Let's try. Uhh." I blew my nose one last time and got my nerve up again and said, "When we get back, would you mind keeping me company tonight? I mean, you told MacDonald you were protecting all us helpless little women, and I let you get away with that bullshit just so as not to spoil your act. I mean, I don't want to impose on you or anything. I'm just trying to help you stay honest."

The grin grew on Lou's face until I thought it would break in two; and finally, when it wouldn't stretch anymore, he said, "Goddamn, woman, I swear, you do drill straight to the heart of things don't you?" He laughed to himself. "Keep me honest. Lord a mercy. You sure you still got enough time for the IHOP?"

"Sure," I told him. "I don't want you running out of food." I walked over and grabbed hold of him. He was big, but I squeezed him like a python. "Just don't dawdle."

INVISIBILITY

The hero's invisibility is not a matter of being seen, but a refusal to run the risk of his own humanity, which [always] involves guilt.[14]

—Ralph Ellison, *The Art of Fiction* No. 8

The boxes Marlow and I brought back from Houston yesterday were stacked neatly in the closet. I had hung up a few things in the bathroom—a skirt, a blouse, and my blazer—to let the wrinkles hang out for today's interview with Caddo Parish schools. My familiar, old workout clothes felt soft and self-indulgent. I had even packed my "Made in Mexico" cotton yoga mat and the little pillow I sit on to meditate. Although the blinds were open, my room was still dark; dawn lay just below the horizon. Getting situated, I used a flashlight to keep from turning on the overhead light and then having to stand up to turn it off again.

The approaching dawn was drawing the temperature up by intervals more subtle than my senses could register while the pecan leaves in the grove beyond my window had emerged from black, then turned from gray to grayish green with the passing minutes. This first rumor of a break from the summer's heat promised what much of the south offers in place of autumn. Not many of the trees would turn red or gold. By late-September, the pecan leaves would be cloaked by webworms, then the leaves would turn brown and join the general leaf fall.

My mind's slow predawn movement took up the caterpillars we call "webworms." A boyfriend once taught me that if I shouted close to them, they would stand up. He claimed that his deeper voice worked better than mine, but I think he was wrong. We would get silly drinking wine or smoking

---

[14.] Ralph Ellison, *Ralph Ellison, The Art of Fiction* No. 8. Interviewed by Alfred Chester and Vilma Howard. *The Paris Review.* No. 8, Spring 1955.

marijuana, then shouting at the webworms for what seemed like hours until they no longer made us laugh. Then one day, I happened to wonder if they might be standing up because the sound vibrations caused them pain, despite their lack of a central nervous system. I never could find a definitive answer, but as Adler would have said, "the spit was in the soup"; and I couldn't shake off the image of myself as feckless tormentor, so that ended that. I never could bring myself to shout at webworms again. But the experience was embedded in my brain, waiting to reappear whenever pecan trees or webworms occurred to me.

And just so, in that slowly evolving morning, I was in the mood for meditation. I had only recently learned to meditate, but when I remembered to do it, I continued to marvel at how clear and confident I felt afterward. That hopeful morning on the heels of my week of relapse, with a promise of new, cooler weather soon to come, felt like the natural time to begin again. I had decided to give it a try for thirty minutes, before tracking down Lou for a practical conversation.

My internal body scan finds some tense areas—stomach, back, shoulders. I can allow those to melt now. Anxiety in the jaw, probably from the Klan's threat. I'll take a few seconds to recognize and accept the feeling then watch it thin out like mist . . . and disappear. Haven't sat cross-legged on the floor in over two weeks. Hips know it. Recognize circulation loss in the lower legs.

Soothe the mind.

Now for the breath. There it is . . . slow, deep.

Yes . . .

Loving-kindness today. Definitely. Much to accept.

Breathe.

Image of Klansmen in robes, burning torches, rags dipped in kerosene and set ablaze. Kerosene will always smell like anger, and anger will always smell like fear. Tightness in my shoulders and back. My push back against anger. Regenerates the anxiety it grew from. Remember R-A-I-N: Recognize it, Allow it, Investigate it, Not be it.

Breathe. Returning from thoughts. Accept. Give myself loving-kindness.

> *May I be filled with loving-kindness.*
> *Breathe.*
> *May I be safe from dangers, inside and out.*
> *Breathe.*
> *May I be well in body and mind.*
> *Breathe.*
> *May I be at ease and happy.*

Breathe.
Firm the belly . . . Breathe.
Marlow is a handsome kid. Funny. Smart. Comfortable to travel with like his Uncle Lou, but more compact in word, deed, and body. Driving me in his pickup to Houston and back—a good chance to know him better—and I needed the help moving. Lou had joked about it, but that's just the way Lou is. I knew he was pleased.
Returning to the breath. Back from thinking Now. Softening. Eyes closing . . . unfocusing.
Breathe . . . allow the drop-off into the Other . . . sounds transforming. Hint of white light . . . maybe to come.
Concealing gown, implicit evil of the Klan. Soiling all they touch.
Breathe . . . back from thinking . . . releasing judgment. Accepting. Breathe. Body speaking: problem in right hip and back.
Breathe. Recognize and allow . . .
Breathe.
Breathe.
Physical attraction to Lou. Last night's comfort. Post-coital glow. How long had it been?
Breathe. Notice and release the thinking. Accept the feeling.
Loving-kindness for Lou:

> *May you be filled with loving-kindness, dear man.*
> *Breathe.*
> *May you be safe from dangers inside and out.*
> *Breathe.*
> *May you be well in body and mind.*
> *Breathe.*
> *May you be at ease and happy.*

Breathe . . . straighten the neck. Firm the belly. Release.
Right hip. Let it resolve. Lower right leg. Pain above pelvis. Allow the pain. Breathe . . . back. Let the senses explore it.
Am I setting us up for violence here? With my self-indulgence? Not about me. Just observing. Up close.
Breathe back from thinking. Release the trapezius.
Settling down to . . . sandy floor of ocean . . . sensing the rocking. Warm saltwater supporting me.
Settling. Breathe . . . float
Light from the surface filtering down.
Breathe.

Loving-kindness for Henry MacDonald—his slender, nervous, sharp-featured face:

> *May you be filled with loving-kindness.*
> *Breathe.*
> *May you be safe from dangers inside and out.*
> *Breathe.*
> *May you be well in body and mind.*
> *Breathe.*
> *May you be at ease and happy.*

Breathe. Peaceful. Easy.
Easy loving-kindness for Cindy . . .

> *Dear Cindy, may you be filled with loving-kindness.*
> *Breathe.*
> *May you be safe from dangers inside and out.*
> *Breathe.*
> *May you be well in body and mind.*
> *Breathe.*
> *May you be at ease and happy.*

Breathe now . . . release it. Don't be it.

> *Cindy as new mother. Contact you today about visiting.*
> *After the school appointment. Let me stop thinking now. Listen more; be attuned. Be open.*

Breathe. Going inside again.
May I be safe. May I learn from those I love. Be attuned. Back.
Back to breathing. Drop thinking gently . . . there now. Stay. Hold.
Flickers of white. Coming.
Breathe.
Be open. Be open. Be open.
Nothing . . . nothing . . . nothing.

I gradually reentered the peaceful room. Saffron streaks across a mottled gray sky. Now I could see clearly without artificial light. The window was open, and I felt a slight breeze. Slightly cooler.

Thank you. Thank you. Thank you.

In the midst of my clearheadedness, I decided to make some notes about what I have to do today and got out my notepad and pen, and sat outside by the picnic table in the cool morning.

Check with Lou on residence, etc.
Open bank account

10:00 AM, Mrs. Sterling, *Caddo Parish Schools*
(check address and phone)

At Caddo Parish schools—find out about reciprocity from Texas.

Other details—getting syllabus, certification, pay, schedule, room, people to meet.

Call Gerald

Confirm connection with Cindy.

Maybe invite Lou and Marlow out to dinner.
(After café closes—if anything is open.)

I wandered across the yard to the kitchen to see if I could get a snack from Elvira and ran into Lou working in the walk-in cooler. I went in and shut the door and got a morning hug and smooch.

"You look great in sweats," he said lightly.

Instinctively, I preened. "These are my yoga clothes."

"Look like sweats to me. You sore from moving yesterday?"

"Poor Marlow," I said. "He carried everything, and today, he had to work."

"How big is your house?"

"Four bedrooms. He slept in the guest room."

"Must have been strange for him too."

"I think it was . . . a little, but Gerald wasn't there. He would have to know I probably would have somebody with me to help me load the truck, so I assume he decided to extend his vacation with Cindy and Robert."

"What else do you have to do?"

"HR interview. New bank account. Post office for a change of address. Eventually, I'll have to reregister the car. That's about it. Have you thought about renting me the room?"

He looked at me for a moment. "Not really. Let's talk when you get your stuff done."

I walked out into the kitchen. Elvira wasn't there. But realizing that I was familiar enough with it, I made myself a piece of toast and warmed a cup of coffee. "You want anything?" I called in to Lou, enjoying the domesticity.

"No. There's some cold oatmeal in that pot if you want it."

I warmed a bowl of oatmeal and milk and sat down at the big table to eat. The new memory of using the kitchen as if I belonged there joined the growing meaning of the place. Strangely enough, the place feeling was already becoming more layered than my childhood home ever felt. Certainly more so than the house I shared with Gerald and Cindy. Maybe that was part of the distance from Cindy. Maybe part of the cause. I know we didn't *try* to make it like that. But how did it happen?

Maybe I could bring her here to demystify my life for her. Probably would be too much at this point for her to see me carrying on with Lou, old enough to be my daddy. I wondered if her childhood felt to her anything like the way it was beginning to feel to me. Probably. Maybe something we could talk about. Maybe change the memory a little while making new ones.

I washed out my cup and bowl and stacked them to dry by the big sink then went back out through the grove to Lou's office and dialed Cindy's number. She sounded sleepy when she answered. I asked her if I had awakened her.

After a pause, she said, "Yes, I guess so. I was dozing after nursing Emily."

I apologized and offered to call later.

"No. No," she said quickly. "I need to get moving."

"So how is Emily?" I asked, trying to remember if I had asked after the baby when I called before.

"Oooh . . ." Cindy said dreamily, sweetly. "She's *wonderful!* She smiled at me this morning. She's so much more alert. And what? Engaged with things?"

I was transported back to when Cindy was that age and when I was seeing her beginning to develop in that way. On the phone, I told her what I was thinking; and she replied quickly, a slight catch in her throat, "Oh, Mother. Was I *really* like this? Did you feel toward me like I feel for her now?"

I felt myself suddenly in deep, uncharted water—almost literally experiencing it with my body—as though my mind were not up to the task. The rush of emotion stole my breath for a few seconds, and I felt tears welling up. "Cindy," I began, but my throat blocked anything more. I was momentarily fearful that I wouldn't be able to catch my breath or that I might sob out loud.

Finally, I apologized and told her that I needed a moment or two to compose myself. "Oh, Mother . . ." Cindy said again.

We laughed, and each of us cried a little until we both were able to speak normally. Then without premeditation, I said, "I would really, really like to come see you and Emily and Robert as soon as possible. I'm not sure, but I think I may be able to get a job teaching in Shreveport in a couple of weeks, so it would be best for me if I could come right away."

"In Shreveport?" Cindy cried. "What on earth?"

"Yes, well, have you talked to your father? I mean, about him and me and all?"

"A little. Why? Are y'all breaking up or something?"

"Well, I can't say for sure. He and I haven't talked about that in detail yet. But for right now, I'm thinking very seriously about staying in Shreveport near Granma."

"Is Shreveport close to Granma's?"

"Less than two hours away, an hour closer than you are to Gainesville."

Cindy went quiet for a while, then she said, "Wow, that's a lot to take in."

"I know it must be, sweetheart. It is for me and your dad too. Is he still there, by the way?"

"You just missed him. He left early this morning. That's why I was napping. He and Robert went into Tallahassee yesterday so Daddy could buy a car. I guess you didn't know that."

"No, but I assumed he would because I have the Pontiac, and I'm going to need to keep it. He'll probably sell the old Plymouth when he gets home. It's on its last legs."

"Yeah, well that's y'all's business."

"Of course it is, dear, and I don't mean to draw you into our affairs in any way, unless y'all should happen to want the old car, though you probably wouldn't need the expense of keeping it up." In the background, I heard the baby fretting, so we made a couple of one-liners about infantile imperatives. I told her I would get off the phone and look forward to speaking to her tomorrow. She didn't have a number for me, so I gave her the motel's business number.

Then just so she would know I was serious, I added, "I hope you'll get a chance to talk to Robert soon, so y'all can figure out when it would be convenient for me to drive over for a couple of days."

"We will. I'll talk to him tonight."

"Great. I have an interview this morning with the Caddo Parish schools about the job, and afterward, I'll be in and out, so just leave me a message on the motel phone when you can, and I'll call back. Everybody here knows who you are, and I'll let them know I'm expecting to hear from you."

There was hesitation in Cindy's voice, and my throat immediately squeezed. I wondered if I had pushed too hard.

"I'll do that, Mother," she said at last. "Robert had to drive back over to Gainesville today to meet with his committee and use the library, so he probably won't be back until late, so it will be tomorrow morning before I call you, okay?"

I told her, "Sure."

Then there was another pause, and she said, "Oh, Mother, I'm so glad you called and that you're coming to see us. You sound so much better today. I can't wait to see you. Emily and I love you."

After hanging up, I sat quietly for a while, my body fairly humming with goodwill and contentment.

Sitting there, feeling safe with my guard down, I was visited by an image that had been recurrent since my father's death, from the reception after his funeral. I remembered my mother perched on the edge of her own sofa with nobody talking to her as though she were in a train station—erect, graceless, uncomfortably costumed, and wearing an awkward hat. Indecisively, I watched her, wanting to approach her, but I couldn't catch her eye. She was completely inward, closed off, privately stricken.

Although I yearned to comfort her, my imagination faltered at resting an arm on her shoulders, which suddenly seemed painfully narrow. An awful lassitude of indecision overtook me, and it deepened the longer I failed to move. Eventually, I wrenched my eyes from her guiltily and went looking for something else to do—to wash out the desire.

What I now recalled was that I found Gerald after the funeral in my parents' kitchen, talking to Mother's brother's wife, Maydell. He was relaxed as always in his public persona, chuckling over what I was sure was a discrete joke. I ducked into the hall and drifted into my parents' bedroom.

As always, I was struck by her precision placing of everything—curtains, blinds, bedspread, furniture—and by the sparseness of articles on polished surfaces. I knew she loathed bric-a-brac, and there wasn't any here—no photographs; nothing cheap or frivolous. The dark, shiny varnish of my dad's hairbrushes stood out on top of the dark bureau. Alone among the other objects in the room, they brought to mind the feeling of his strong presence. I could almost smell his cigarettes and aftershave. Hesitantly, I lifted my hand to one of the brushes but paused short of it. For that moment, the brush was as though too powerfully mysterious to fathom. My hand hovered over it as I felt a longing in my throat for something, though the image of what eluded me, a connection just out of reach.

"Do you need something?" Though not unkindly, Mother's voice gave me a startle of trespass, as though I had been discovered violating a space at once sanctified and sanctioned.

"No, ma'am," I replied automatically, checking my posture.

The taste of intimacy with Cindy on the telephone had evoked something about that interlude, the remembrance of a longing too late recognized, I suppose, and the mortal melancholy it entailed. I thought back to the humming sense of goodwill following the phone call with Cindy and realized how rarely those experiences had occurred. I almost gasped at the thought of this child of mine having lived her entire life with the same resigned yearning for an attuned parental connection irrevocably unrequited that I had.

Meanwhile, I had more things to do, although I wouldn't spoil it by telling Cindy that. I checked my watch and realized that I would have to hurry to make my appointment. Happily, the wrinkles had smoothed out of my clothes overnight. And I didn't have to spend time worrying about what to wear. I entered the shower gratefully, full of hope and purpose.

When I came out of the interview a couple of hours later, I could feel the adrenaline singing in my ears. Thinking back over the morning, I smiled to myself and thought, *If you want to nail a job interview, arrange to have your kid tell you she loves you just before you go in for it.* As confident as I had been, the actual tentative offer of a job had made it seem official, and I was flying and fending off my old familiar fear of failing.

Before the usual second-guessing arrived, though, I figured I had time to capitalize on the momentum and my feeling of strength by paying one last visit to Henry MacDonald to maybe seal up that old dragon in his emotional cave. I parked in front of the drugstore and went in. Millie, his lone salesclerk, still in uniform, with "Millie" embroidered with red thread above her left breast, was busy a couple of aisles away; and the soda jerk was still behind the counter. I quipped to myself wryly that maybe they were chained to their posts and imagined them running on little invisible rails embedded in the floor.

I climbed onto a stool and smiled at the soda jerk. Though I had expected my presence to make him nervous, when he walked over to me and asked if he could help me, I was humbled to realize that he had not even recognized me. Amazing what a little makeup and a skirt and blazer can do. I ordered a piece of apple pie and a cup of coffee.

To my relief, he served me without hesitation. Meanwhile, I noticed Millie had turned her back and was hurrying away into what I had come to think of as the dark recesses of the store, where I remembered MacDonald's office was located. I faced down a flash of anxiety, although on the whole, I was calmer than before. I took a deep breath and slowed my breathing, mentally getting my legs under me.

MacDonald came out looking tentative, his head swiveling on the slender stalk of his neck. *Probably as freaked as I am*, I thought. He greeted me formally as "Mrs. Stallings," but I purposely addressed him as "Henry" to keep the power on.

"What can I do for you?" he asked finally.

"Nothing special," I said. "I just wanted to test the water and decided to get some pie and coffee in the process to see if the boy would serve me this time." He colored slightly and looked around the store then slid onto a stool next to me. The soda jerk made a move to come back, but MacDonald waved him off. Finally, MacDonald looked around again, ran his finger under his collar, and said in a very low voice, "I think we can talk here without being overheard. What was it you wanted to check on?"

I studied him for a few moments. He had missed a few whiskers on his upper lip, and he was maybe breathing more heavily than normal. I was surprised to notice a slight twitch under his left eye that I couldn't remember having seen before, and the pulse in his throat may have been a little fast, but I hadn't paid much attention to it before. Otherwise, he seemed composed.

Finally, I said, "Okay, I guess first of all, I was hoping we could normalize things between us a little because we *are* neighbors, at least for a while, but I guess that will take care of itself. And by the way, Lou says the breakfast went just fine. What did you think?

"It was interesting, he said noncommittally.

I asked him if they planned to meet again. He said he thought so but didn't know for sure. I couldn't figure out whether it was fear or anger or what that I was picking up from him but didn't have time to worry about it. I told him I hoped it would work out, so we could all relax a little.

"Speaking of which," I said, "there's some things I wanted to clarify with you after the conversation with you and me and Lou that may help us wind down. Okay?"

He nodded and I said, "Good. First of all, I want to make clear to you that I have no intention of suing you or anything like that for the things you did the other day. I mean, I'm guessing that now that you know who I am, you're not going to feel threatened by me or anything, so there wouldn't be any need for it. You can relax as long as you play straight with me. Okay?"

He started a denial, but I cut him off, telling him that I hadn't come in to start an argument. He fell silent, so I waited for a while and finally added, "So can you accept that?" He nodded but still looked perturbed. I was frustrated that he was not responding very much, and I couldn't gauge how he was taking what I said. After a silence though, I decided to just push on into what I had started.

"Okay, so next thing is this: I know I let Louis Fontinot do most of the talking yesterday, but I want it to be clear that he does not speak for me, nor does anybody else—except possibly Sheriff Odum or my lawyer. I guess what I want to say is, I didn't sic Lou on you. He is a friend but not my protector. I think I can pretty well take care of myself.

"You just happened to catch me at a disadvantage when you refused to serve me and then pushed me, but I don't plan to let that happen again. So if you have any more issues with me about this whole thing, or if anything new should come up or you get worried that I might be in cahoots with the demonstrators, I would appreciate it if you would bring up your concerns with me, not Lou. Okay?" He nodded again, maybe a little more relaxed.

"Okay, one last thing. There is a possibility that I may be staying in Caddo Parish, and if that happens, I probably would be moving to Shreveport."

"Congratulations," he said in what struck me as his first approach to friendliness.

"Thank you," I said. "It's not final yet. The reason I stopped by is that, the last time we talked, you had several misconceptions about me and what I was or was not doing the night of the sit-in. Is all that cleared up now? Are you satisfied that I did not, in any way, participate in the sit-in? By the way, I never got a chance to ask you what made you think there was going to be another sit-in at your place. Did you get a tip or a warning or something?"

He seemed to ponder his reply for a long time. "Well, now," he said finally, "I don't know anybody that saw you in the H-E-B, but a bunch of people saw you hanging around with those white boys that was staying at the motel."

"Just what do you mean by 'hanging around'?" I snapped, feeling a surge of anger.

He smirked. "How would I know what all goes on over at that motel?" he said. "Besides sitting around in the backyard and talking and giggling, I mean? But from what I heard, y'all were pretty thick over there during the daytime."

I could hear the insinuations and knew instinctively how they would sound when he was with his buddies. I took a couple of deep breaths to keep my voice steady. "Okay, Henry, I don't care for your tone or what I infer to be your insinuations, but there is one thing you need to understand. I have already spoken to an attorney, and I acquainted him with the circumstances and the events and your mistaken assumption that I was involved in it. I have also given him the names of several witnesses who are willing to testify that I had nothing to do with it."

I was lying about seeing the lawyer, but I figured he wouldn't be able to find that out. "So," I went on, "I just wanted to give you a heads up that if that baseless story continues to circulate, the sheriff and his deputy and all of them will assume it's coming from you."

"You can't prove that, and you can't leave that hanging over my head," he said belligerently.

"I understand perfectly because that's exactly what you are doing to me," I told him mock agreeably. "I would prefer that the story would never be heard again, and I give you my word that I won't strike the first blow. That's a promise. But I hope you're clear that I am more than willing to strike the last blow if I have reason to believe you are still spreading that lie.

"The rest is up to you," I said evenly. And you should keep in mind that I have been assured by my lawyer that I have all the proof I need to establish a case if I should need to file suit against you for libel, slander, or aggravated assault. Oh, and one more thing you should know," I added. "Strictly as a precaution, I have given Sheriff Odum a sealed affidavit to be opened in case anything further happens to me. It sets out in detail what happened here at the drugstore and a list of who saw it, including the sheriff's deputy, who has apologized and told me that he would back me up if need be."

At least the last part was mostly true. Odum *had* assured me that he had had what he called a "come to Jesus" talk with his deputy, Lonnie. Nonetheless, walking back to my room, I was shaking pretty hard with anger as much as fear. I didn't much want to go inside, but there was nowhere else that I could think of going to work off my adrenaline.

I was pleased to see Marlow step out of the kitchen. He greeted me with the shyness he had shown since our trip to Houston. I asked him if he was ready to start school. He laughed and shook his head. "I guess you could say I'm of many minds about it," he said ruefully. "Like I was telling you on the trip, I look forward to being 'in college,' but I'm still not quite sure what that means. I guess you might say I'm pretty sure *who* I am, but not who I'm *going* to be."

This was a conversation we had already wrestled with while riding in his truck. Referring to his quandary, I laughed and let it go, angry at myself because I couldn't help thinking of what a Henry MacDonald could make of my laughing with Marlow. I wondered if he knew we had traveled out of town together yesterday or spent the night at my house in Houston.

I nodded to Marlow, and we fell silent. "Yeah, well," I said finally, "I empathize, but at least you are beginning the journey."

"Right, and I like what you said about college being a kind of reprieve before full adulthood."

"But it still doesn't save you from the ambivalence now, right?" Then remembering what I had meant to say, I asked, "Listen, what are you doing for dinner tonight?"

"I'm working," he said. "Probably pick up something here in the kitchen, why?"

"Oh, I was going to invite you and your Uncle Lou out for Mexican food as a 'thank you' for all your help."

"Well, thanks, but Uncle Lou's cooking anyway. Elvira's spending the night in Natchitoches."

"Well, show's how much I know." I gave him a peck on the cheek. "Okay. That's an IOU for Mexican food."

Lou and Marlow closed the café at ten o'clock. I had helped them put away things and wash the few remaining dirty dishes while Marlow swept and Lou straightened the cooler. The three of us stood in the pecan grove and said, "Good night." Marlow appeared content to keep chatting and to come into Lou's office for a while, but Lou and I sort of hemmed and hawed around for a while until Marlow figured out we might need to talk privately or something, and told us good night. As he drove out of the parking lot, Lou and I went into the office. Four of the cottages were rented that night, so the office was pretty public.

Lou held open the door to his room, and I went in. The place was neat as ever. I marveled again that as many books lined the walls of his room as lined the walls of his office. I sat on the couch and he joined me and asked almost shyly what I wanted to do about sleeping arrangements. Feeling shy myself, and not quite ready to commit to another evening, I dodged the question, reminding him we still had things to talk about. He asked what was left, and I said first of all, we needed to talk about Henry MacDonald.

"That's right," Lou said, "You saw him today, didn't you?"

I nodded, and Lou suggested that we wait until tomorrow morning and then asked what else?

"All right," I said, "but just for the record, I still don't trust him. I think he could be dangerous, and we had a pretty rough exchange today."

"Anything new about that?" he asked, suddenly alert.

I shook my head. "Nothing concrete, it's just that I still pick up a strong feeling of anger and fear off of him, a sort of sulkiness ready to turn to anger." I thought for a minute. "He clearly dislikes me because I'm a woman and speak up to him, and because I'm a stranger and because I 'hung around,' as he puts it, with the protesters. He insinuates that I flirted with them or worse, but that probably goes for any female who threatens him . . . And when I look directly into his eyes, he looks away, usually down—and of course, his open, unabashed racial hatred."

"Okay," Lou said. "We need to figure how to handle him. Let's work on that in the morning, all right with you?" He laid his arm on the back of the couch behind me and asked, "So how're you feeling about you and me now?"

"Well," I said, "at the risk of seeming ungrateful, I still haven't figured out what made you decide to pull your little stunt that night when Gerald and I stopped here."

"Yeah, that," he said.

It's crucial to me," I told him, "and the more time we spend together, the more worrisome it becomes."

He was quiet for so long that I began to feel uncomfortable. But finally, he cleared his throat. "I've been wondering about that myself." He said seriously. "A lot, and I know I'm overdue apologizing to you, mostly because I haven't figured out what to say."

"Okay," I said. "How about I start with a question or two?"

"Please," he said gratefully.

"Okay. First, did you interpret anything I did that night as flirting with you?"

He shook his head. "Not in the least."

I must have looked perplexed.

"No, it wasn't anything you done. It was me, and besides, I'm not so dense that I'd try to justify it. I am ashamed and embarrassed. Marlow almost quit over it, and Elvira is just now getting back to where she doesn't treat me like a bad cold." He stood up and walked around the room for a while.

"So do you remember what led up to it?" I asked him finally.

"Well, for one thing, I had a couple of drinks that night."

I must have looked skeptical because he hurried to add, "Not like I had a couple of drinks and went crazy, but like my sense of myself got off center that night, so I poured a couple of shots of whisky into myself—I guess just to crank it up some more. Did you know I have just about given up drinking?"

I asked him if he has those attacks or relapses or whatever he calls them very often. "Because if you do," I said, "I'll have to figure out some kind of early warning system, or else I won't be able to stay here."

He was shamefaced. "That's fair," he said. "I wouldn't blame you."

"And you know I'm not preaching or being holier than thou or anything because you know about my little number last week, right?"

He nodded and then stared at his hands.

"So can you let me in on what you were thinking?" I asked, mostly just to fill the space.

"I guess so. But remember, this is not about justification. It's just a description, okay?"

I nodded.

"All right, here goes. Damn, this sounds stupid, but here it is. I somehow got it into my head on the strength of, what? Twenty minutes of the barest acquaintance with you. Uhh . . . that I saw something in you that made me feel like I 'knew' you, and even that you might sort of know me. Almost a kind of kinship, it seemed."

I couldn't help laughing. "Yeah?" I said, "Well let me tell you. Where I come from, if what you were feeling that night was kinship, then we're talking incest."

"You know what I mean."

"No, I'm afraid I don't."

"All right," he said. "It wasn't just that you're good looking and all. That wouldn't have done it. It was more the way you *seemed* toward me. Like somebody that was . . . 'Hungry' isn't the word I want. More like I believe you are a person of strong appetites. Damn, this sounds cheesy. An appetite for life . . . what a fucking cliché that is! But also the sense that you had always denied that about yourself, maybe even to yourself." He finished in a rush, flushing under his permanent tan. "Now that's just clear as mud, isn't it?" he continued, as if to cover his embarrassment.

I waited, curious to know where this was going to take him and not wanting to get in the way. But after a few minutes, when he didn't say anything, I offered, "I'm giving you the benefit of the doubt that you are not saying you thought I was an easy . . . what? *Conquest*—I guess they used to say."

He shook his head almost violently. "No, not that at all," he protested.

"Well," I said, "to be brutally honest, what you've just told me sounds like just another run-of-the-mill narcissistic sexist fantasy, and frankly, I'm disappointed. But those things happen, I guess, even to thoughtful people, and you say you *are* trying to be honest. But what worries me, and what I've been wanting most of all to ask, is: Was there something about me that made you suspect I was an alcoholic?"

"Well, maybe not quite that," he said. "I don't believe that 'alcoholic personality' stuff you hear at the AA meetings, and besides, you said you hadn't had a drink in several months."

"You're sure you didn't see me that way?"

"Yeah, but you *did* look like you were no stranger to pain and fear—just plain human stuff, nothing psycho, but maybe a little more painful than most."

I wasn't sure what he meant, and it must have shown.

"Like you might be willing"—he paused, shifting his weight on the couch nervously—"to risk pain in order to get something you thought was really important."

"I guess you mean that as a compliment," I said half humorously.

"Yeah, I do," he said, grinning, "because that's where this 'kinship' thing comes in. That sort of describes me too. We seem to have it in common. I mean, there was just this nonsensical thought—not even a belief, just a kind of passing daydream—that in spite of the difference in our ages and education and all, I could imagine you noticing me, *seeing* me, if you will, behind the busted-up face and all the rest.

"Because crazy as it sounds, I felt this mindless premonition that you would like me if you could get to know me. I hadn't been with anyone in years. I didn't even know if I could be close to a woman, especially not somebody like you. But the fantasy had it that somehow or another, we might find a way to be together."

He trailed off lamely, but I told him I thought I understood.

"So you suddenly decided that you could just dope up my coffee and grab my tit and I would fall in love with you?"

"Damn," he said finally, "that sounds subhuman when you describe it like that. And I guess that's how it really was."

We fell silent again, and I leaned against him without realizing it. Finally, Lou said cautiously, "Do you think my doing that made you relapse?" When he said that, I let my memory go back to that night and then was shocked to be re-experiencing the actual panic that had followed his groping me. The new memory was a lot stronger than the way I had been remembering it. It frightened me to re-experience it that way, and my first impulse was to tell him to change the subject. But somehow I knew that if I didn't let the recall happen and get on the other side, I would have to walk away and not look back. And I wasn't ready to do that. So I told him that in one blurt.

"But I want you to know that I am not blaming you for my relapse. I had all kinds of bad stuff chasing itself around in me, the stuff about Cindy and all, and in the process, I had to confront a lot of shit about my feelings for Gerald. I had to admit to myself that I had never loved him from the get-go. I was just in an adolescent haze about the romance of getting pregnant by a guy who was going off to war. Gerald's a nice guy and all, but under normal circumstances, I would never for a minute have considered marrying him; and truth be known, I suspect that in normal times, he wouldn't have married me either. Probably I was too wild and he was too tame."

I laughed—pretty bitterly, I guess—and added, "And then the poor bastard crashed his airplane and never got into the war after all.

"But to answer your question, the straight answer is I don't know. I think that I would have relapsed eventually if I never got that stuff straightened out in my head. At the worst, you probably just gave the ball a hefty shove."

He walked over to the window and looked out for a while. Then finally, he said without looking around, "All right, but I think I need to know as best I can how it felt to you."

I already had a hunch it was finally going to come around to that and was a little ahead of him. "Okay, Lou," I told him, "if you want me to, I'll do my best to give you a complete account, although I'm not sure how completely I remember. Parts of it are pretty sketchy. But let me tell you one thing, this is costing me, and I wouldn't put up with this if I didn't think a lot of you. Do you understand that?"

He nodded, looking nervous as a deer in a clearing. I saw him uncross his legs and plant his feet on the floor as if unconsciously preparing to withstand a blow—either that or fixing to run, I didn't know which.

"At first," I said, allowing the feelings to flood back in and clearing my throat. "At first I didn't taste the booze in my coffee, although I had already caught you peeping down the front of my shirt, so I just took a big swallow to cover my anger and act like I didn't give a shit. But then as soon as I swallowed and tasted the booze, I knew I was in trouble.

"Because you must have felt taken advantage of, right?"

"That and because I had not had anything to drink in several months, and I was pinning my being able to reconcile with Cindy on my having been totally free of booze for five months. It was all just hearsay with Cindy because I hadn't seen her in all that time, so I was hoping to appear to her to be a completely changed person and maybe even a good and loving mother."

I considered that for a minute and said, "And right! But wait, you're not off the hook yet. When you say 'taken advantage of,'" I said with all the mockery and contempt I could drive into the expression, "that doesn't scratch the surface, Louis. Symbolically, you *raped* me. Do you understand that?" I paused to let that sink in. "You might just as well have just hauled off and jammed something up into me. Can you take that in?"

He nodded, looking straight at me with pain in his eyes.

"I was defenseless and totally unsuspecting, and you didn't say, 'Please, ma'am, kiss my ass' or anything. You just poured a bunch of bourbon into my coffee and let me swallow it, and then the next thing I knew, you had stood me up to pose for my husband to take our picture, and I'll be damned if you didn't grab on to my tit and squeeze the hell out of it and then make me stand there before God and everybody while you showed me off!"

Feeling the fear and anger surge over me again, I panicked and stood up and literally began to feel nauseated and weak all over again, and I began to tremble violently.

But I continued to talk. I told Lou, "Then when you squeezed my breast, I felt trapped," I said a little more quietly. "I was terrified—and desperate to escape, but when you let go of me, I all of a sudden felt unmoored."

Saying that, I had begun to shiver so violently that my teeth almost chattered. He put his arm around my shoulder and pulled me up against his side.

"Can you follow what I'm telling you?" I asked. He nodded, grim faced; and I sat there, leaning against him, the tremors slowing slightly. "And I was standing there, swaying and panting, and from somewhere far off, I'll swear I could like hear something like a tiny, tin-sounding recording of my own voice, as though it was narrating my life. 'It is two eighteen in the morning,' it said, 'and I am standing here breathless in some godforsaken café on the edge of fucking Shreveport, Louisiana.'"

I leaned back against the back of the couch and went on more quietly still and looking up at him, I said, "With that voice almost imitating my own and drowning out everything else that was going on, it was as if I couldn't find myself. The panic deepened, sharpened. Then somewhere in there, I had this weird sense that I couldn't decide how to compose my face. It felt as though, for all I knew, my face might on its own be making hideous grins or grimaces without my volition.

"Some of the customers had seen the whole incident, and I swear I could still track their reactions across *their* faces—surprise, amusement, lechery. Marlow, though of course I didn't know him then, had stepped out through the kitchen door moments before you let me go. He stopped in mid-stride, the poor guy, and leaned on the push broom he had been carrying.

"He looked confused, and then almost as horrified as I was, like he had never seen something like that—at least not something you were doing—so that I had an incongruous urge to *comfort* him, of all things, soften his wide eyes in the middle of my own terror.

"Just then, I was surprised to feel my heart beat grow *heavier* like I couldn't hold myself up straight. You know?"

"Not quite," he said miserably, "but go on."

I looked at him more closely. Tears were running down his cheeks. "I can't think of any other way to describe it," I told him. "But anyway, on top of that reaction, then this other thing intruded that I have been suffering for a while now—the room suddenly seemed to fly off into the distance with an almost audible rushing *sigh*, shrinking you and Gerald and the dozen or so spectators who had witnessed my humiliation—including Marlow—to less than doll-size. I remember thinking, 'Oh no! I don't need that shit now!'"

"You mean you had a hallucination?" Lou asked, deeply perturbed.

"Not quite," I said. "The scene was unchanged, but it was like I'm looking through a zoom lens, and everything just zooms away. I don't see things that aren't there, just everything distorted and far away."

Lou wiped his eyes with his sleeve. "Is that frightening?" he asked. "It would scare the hell out of me."

"It used to me too," I told him, feeling completely calm now in the slow-moving aftermath of the remembered experience, "but not so much anymore. I can almost predict when it's going to happen, basically when I get stressed out. That night though, it was just one more blow, like being hit one more time on a sore place," I said.

"I had learned a while back that sometimes if I can pick out one person to make eye contact with, the mutual focus or something seems to return the scene to normal. I turned back to Marlow to connect with him, but he was looking at you and didn't see me.

"The pounding of my heart increased. The odd thought actually crossed my mind, 'One hundred and forty beats, moving to one hundred sixty.' And that was so terrifying that I couldn't bear any longer *not* to run. I stepped around the front tables, by that time trying *not* to look at anyone, for fear of being propelled into some sort of emotional overdrive.

"But as I should have expected, as soon as I made that decision and started my move, Marlow looked up, and we momentarily locked eyes after all. I was struck by his curly copper hair and serious eyes, which always seem to be interested in everything they see. He looked younger somehow than he looks now, two weeks later, wearing that apron around his skinny hips.

"He was looking at me intently as though trying to see inside me. I remember a delusional moment when I gasped because I thought he might actually be one of my senior math students magically transported to Shreveport for summer vacation. Of course, I recognized the absurdity of that immediately. Still, I remember remarking to myself on the earnestness of Marlow's expression, 'My lord,' I remember thinking, 'that boy wants to make my acquaintance!'"

Lou said bleakly, "Well, you summed *him* up all right. Upset him so much he didn't come back to work for a week."

"Yeah, so I heard."

"Well, anyway," I said, "my panic eased a little when the room turned back to normal. I caught a rush of embarrassment that drenched my face in sweat. I broke my connection with Marlow's eyes and avidly examined the floor, and at that moment, I was shocked to find myself struggling to keep a straight face against a threatening nervous giggle welling up in me and telling myself *now* in a familiar, cold censuring voice, 'Don't you dare laugh, Lillian. If you so much as crack a smile, every one of them will think the worst, and you will be mortified for life!'

"That actually got me moving again. I finally pushed clear of the tables and headed straight for the exit, desperate to outrun my terror. I tried to run slowly, taking care not to trip or stumble. Gerald was kneeling by the door, oblivious to everything. Dodging around him, I actually heard him humming as he packed up his camera gear. Poor dear—he didn't have a clue!

"I felt a blast of anger blow through me. 'I'm leaving,' I said. 'Now!' It came out sounding to my own ears like the bark of a mad dog, but he gave no sign of having heard me. I hit the door and almost tripped on that one step down to the walkway. My feet reached the shell-covered parking lot, and I began to run. I tasted vomit before I knew it was coming up, so I just leaned over and let fly as quietly as I could into some bushes, trying not to soil my blouse or loafers, hoping nobody saw me. Some of the vomit had gone up my nose—coffee and the unmistakable taste of bourbon."

"So that was the worst of it?" Lou asked, still holding me, stroking my hair.

"Yeah, it was pretty much downhill from there. The car wasn't locked, so I yanked the door open and twisted my hips hard to the left and let them pull me sideways into the passenger seat, banging my head in the process. For a while, I had a pain in my neck and shoulder, but I was mostly intent on pulling my legs in after me and slamming the door. Pretty soon, I heard the car's trunk open, followed by the sounds of Gerald putting his camera equipment away then closing the trunk. He crunched through the crushed shell around to the left side of the car and got in.

"I could feel him peering at me in the dimness of the car. I continued to sit rigidly, staring straight ahead, ignoring him. Unfair as it may seem now, at that moment, I hated him. He asked me if I was okay, and I said I was 'fine.'"

In recounting it to Lou, I had experienced it all again, all of it—the sound of the crushed shell, the bright light in the café and the parking lot, the dimness of the car, the residual pressure on my breast, the taste of bourbon, my anger, my invisibility—all there, overwhelming. I swallowed and wiped tears from my face with my hand but then tried to straighten up. Lou handed me some tissues. I wiped and blew and snuffled.

I buried my head in Lou's chest while a belated violent tremor ran from my feet up my thighs and to the back of my head. I was in its thrall for several seconds, and then it passed, leaving me drained, empty of all feeling. In the ensuing stillness, I realized that Lou was holding me tightly against his chest; and I was hugging him back, grateful for his having passed through it with me.

"What was all that reaction just now?" Lou asked.

"I don't know, but something enormous," I said.

"I could feel it," he said. Then after a minute, he laughed.

"What?" I asked.

"I don't know," he said, "just a bunch of images chasing themselves around inside my mind."

We sat quietly. A breeze came through the windows. Lou turned off all but one of the lamps then came back, and we enjoyed the breeze and the quiet. Occasional traffic sounds came in from the road. The reverie felt mutual.

"Poor Gerald," I said out of nowhere. "He is a thoughtful and pleasant man. Unfailingly, he has been kind to me, but for years, I have felt like I was invisible to him—just as I was to my dad and a lot of other people.

"But I saw you."

"Yeah—you and Marlow and maybe the fish in Robert's tanks." We shared a chuckle. "But I just realized he probably has been just as invisible to me as I am to him. Same with my parents too, I imagine. At times, they must have wondered where the hell I came from."

I relaxed back against him, still unwinding from the tension of the uncoiling memory, which was beginning to feel less threatening—more just a scary story.

"So to go back to your question, I don't know why I drank. Your abuse sort of started the train," I said. "But as I said, I had been furious with Gerald all that day because he had this hidden agenda he hadn't told me about or consulted with me on that had taken us several hundred miles out of our way to see his mother in Lufkin and then my mother in Troup, with long visits each place. We had eaten at both places, and my stomach was upset and a lot of other crap."

"All that, and you were feeling more and more like the *Invisible Man*," Lou offered.

"No!" I almost shouted. "Just invisible. Not Ralph Ellison's character. Sorry for yelling in your ear, but I wouldn't ever have compared myself to him. I haven't earned the right, thank god. I just wanted to be known as myself, that's all"

Suddenly, almost desperate for honesty, I plunged on. "All right," I said. "Here's the last thing I've been holding back. When Cindy told us she was pregnant, it was like somebody had let the air out of my tires. I did *not* want to be a grandmother yet. I was just thirty-seven at the time, and it seemed like the end of my life. I'm ashamed to say that I just couldn't bring myself to make any of the grandmotherly gestures. I didn't attend her baby showers. I didn't chat with her about motherhood or offer to buy baby cribs and all that stuff that mothers of the expectant mothers do. I didn't offer to go to help her when the baby was born. Gerald hinted but didn't say anything directly. He took it upon himself to fill in as many of those blanks as he could.

"Well, as the day approached, a chill grew between Cindy and me where before we had always been pretty close. Then, as the due date approached, two things happened. If Cindy had asked me to come help her, I would have gone, regardless how I felt—but to my chagrin, she didn't invite me. Although to be perfectly honest, I hadn't wanted to go. Still, I was devastated.

"But the real heartbreaker came when I realized that my main feeling was one of relief. By that time, I had convinced myself that I would not be capable of the kind of intuitive, loving interaction with the baby that I knew all species of babies need. Irrational or not, all I felt when Emily was born was terror that I would not be up to handling her. Cindy invited Gerald and me to come for a visit, but that was all, and inwardly, I heaved—as they say—a great guilty sigh of relief."

I looked at Lou. His face was full of concern, but not horror. Then I remembered what Elvira had told me about his marriage. He smiled at me, his face dry now, but his eyes glistening. "You know about that feeling, don't you?" I asked.

"Yep," he replied. "To myself, I called it the failure to become fully human."

I thought about that for a minute and then asked, "Then you know why it's so important to me to rebuild my connection with Cindy and her baby."

"Yep," he repeated.

He stretched, and I snuggled closer to him. With my story told and more completely remembered at that, and with all the ups and downs of the day, I was bone tired.

I was deeply into a sensual dream when the phone rang.

Lou answered the phone and immediately sat up and said, "Are you all okay? Where are you now? Good. What about the kids?" He listened intently for a while and made sympathetic sounds and comments. "Good," he said finally.

Lou's alarm clock said four-oh-six. It was dark outside.

He covered the phone and said quietly, "They firebombed Ada's house. Nobody's hurt. The house burned to the ground, but they were spending the night at Annie's. They're still with her."

Back on the phone, he said, "That must have been terrifying. Could you save anything from the house? Those sons of bitches. So listen, Elvira, just sit tight there. I'm going to phone Bill Odum here so he can coordinate with the sheriff there, and I will call Marie Lynn in case you think of anything else y'all need. I'll be heading for Natchitoches in fifteen minutes."

I stepped in front of Lou and pointed to myself and nodded emphatically. Lou said into the telephone, "Lillian will be coming with me. She wants to speak to you." He handed me the phone and began putting on his clothes.

Elvira's voice was angry but subdued. I asked her about clothing, and she told me where to find clothes for both herself and Ada because everything had been destroyed.

"Do the kids have any clothes in your room?" She told me to check her closet and chest of drawers and bring whatever I found that might be familiar and comforting. I suggested she see if Marie Lynn had any of their stuff we could pick it up, but she pointed out that some stores would be open in a few hours.

I pulled on my jeans and loafers and headed for the kitchen, grateful that I was familiar enough with the kitchen to make a pot of Elvira's chicory coffee and put a pan of milk on to heat. Then I grabbed a big grocery bag and hurried back to get Elvira's room key from Lou.

He was in the office, busy talking on the telephone. A canvas bag lay on the desk. He picked it up and slung it over his shoulder. I could tell he was talking to Marie Lynn. He told her goodbye and asked me if I was sure I wanted to go. I told him that I was, but I would also be glad to stay and open the café and watch the office.

He said that Marie Lynn had already gotten Marlow up, and he would be heading for Shreveport, glad to miss a day of school. "After we get a chance this morning to look it all over and see what needs doing, probably you or I will need to come back here and give him a hand. I asked Lou if he thought

Marlow would be safe, and he smiled and said that he thought so. He seems to have my good-luck genes."

"Okay," I said, but I wanted to drive my car in case we needed to bring people back, since probably nobody had seen my car before, and it wasn't associated with Ada or Elvira. Besides, we could talk on the way.

I asked Lou if he had already spoken to Bill Odum. He said that he had, and I suggested he might want to call back and let Bill know that Henry MacDonald was hostile and was on the verge of threatening when I talked to him yesterday. He nodded and picked up the phone again.

"Oh, and there's a pot of coffee on the stove. And would you turn off the fire under the milk?"

I looked at him and was surprised to see him smiling. "What?" I asked.

He didn't answer but leaned over and kissed me. "Can you handle a pistol?" he asked finally.

I nodded and swallowed. "Daddy taught me how. But I never shot anything but cans and bottles."

"You probably won't need to," he said.

I turned to go to Elvira's room, and he said, "I'll meet you in the garage. You'll be carrying clothes and stuff. I'll bring the coffee."

PART FIVE
Resurrections of Marlow

> If there is something distinctinve about an event—about what constitutes an event and thus has historical value—it is the fact that it is irreversible, that there is always something in it which exceeds meaning and interpretations.[15]
>
> Jean Baudrillard, The Illusion of the End

[15.] Jean Baudrillard. The Illusion of the End, Translated by Chris Turner. (Stanford, California: Stanford University Press) 1994, p 13

Resurrections of Marlow

> *The way we construct our defenses tends to suggest that we unconsciously invite, or sustain contact with, whatever we fear . . . (in the way that sadness, for example, can be a way of reminding ourselves of what's missing in our lives.) As in a neurosis, we are pursuing something by running away from it . . . Once every fear is a wish . . . our fears become the clue to our desires; aversiveness always conceals a lure.*[16]
>
> —Adam Phillips, *Terrors and Experts*

Fading night reveals brush, trees, and buildings along a dirt road on the outskirts of a small town in Southeast Asia. Roadside trees are mostly acacia, varieties of eucalyptus, tamarinds, evergreen araucarias, figs of various kinds, including the sacred bo tree. Their shades of gray alchemize imperceptibly into daylit, many-hued greens of leaves and the many reds, oranges, pinks, yellows, and whites of their flowers. A moist perfume of brine, fish, and seaweed rides a breeze drawn from an unseen sea.

Momentarily, sand and roadside litter spin in a dust devil, which suddenly dances along the road toward the town. Bits of paper return to the ground as the minor disturbance resolves itself in front of a buff-colored temple and an ancient bo tree, silhouetted against the paling sky. Light from flickering candles or lanterns shows through the temple's windows.

Across the road from the temple, a fortresslike, two-story duplex of white concrete is—like the rest of the scene—emerging from darkness as the morning light grows like a three-dimensional image on photosensitive paper. The top apartment is open to the street, its large windows covered only by rusting screen wire.

[16.] Adam Phillips, *Terrors and Experts* (Cambridge, Mass.: Harvard University Press, 1995), 48.

The mouth of an alley opens between the side of the duplex fortress and a compound of lodgings and workshops surrounded by bushes and trees. A few chickens scratch in the yard of the compound. A rooster has just finished crowing, and the ensuing silence hangs in the humid air, backed by a faint and continuous humming discordance of voices, clanks, scrapings, laughter, babies crying, exclamations, dog barks, two-cycle motors running, lowing cattle, shrieks of a desperate pig, the ponderous three-note squeak and crunch of a moving ox cart, and the birdlike trill of a knife-and-scissors sharpener's whistle announcing its owner's readiness to hone all kinds of blades from razors to axes. It is difficult to pick out a single progression of notes to listen to. The fickle ear begins following one tune only to be lured astray by others.

An eight-meter log, a meter in diameter, rests on trestles. Midway down the log, a shirtless man—trouser legs rolled and hitched up above his knees as he squats on his heels on the log's bark—is sliding a bow saw up and down in a cut that goes completely through the log (the blade sticking through the bottom, secured at both ends by the bow). Progressing at the rate of about a millimeter per stroke, the man is patiently ripping a massive timber from the log, destined to form the keel of a new *junk*. The resolute rasp of his sawing lays down a percussive groove into which the other sounds merge occasionally, like the fleeting synchronies of orchestra instruments being tuned for a concert.

The alley is known locally (half humorously) as "Sin Alley." It extends for the equivalent of about four city blocks before giving way to open rural land. The alley is lined with small squatter lodgings constructed of woven bamboo and a variety of other materials—cardboard, packing crate planks bearing English words and phrases, plywood from the same sources, the occasional piece of corrugated metal, canvas, the hood of a military vehicle—most of them leaned against the wall of an ordinary building such as the white duplex.

Something between a museum, a junk heap, and an overturned ant colony, the alleyway is cluttered with people, mostly young women, children, and ancient survivors of outlived lives—old women who peel vegetables, bodies lumped by arthritis; old men with long, sparse, yellowing white beards seemingly communing with other lives if not with other worlds.

Many people in this busy neighborhood are missing parts of themselves—an eye, some fingers, a leg. The diligent sawyer himself lacks a left ear, and the skin on the left side of his face and head is livid and rumpled with burn scars. The left eye does not seem to work quite properly. Nevertheless, his trancelike concentration on his work suggests satisfaction with the scourging bite of the saw.

If you could spy through one of the open windows of the duplex's upper floor, say from the broad upper limbs of the bo tree, you might see a man sprawled on a bed in the weak morning light. He seems to be asleep, but up close, you could see muscles bunching up in the forearm, jaw, and shoulder. His head is covered with a wild bush of copper-colored ringlets. One eye has just popped open next to the pillow. Its line of sight traverses a landscape of disarranged sheets to where a naked girl is reaching for something beside the bed.

The voyeur on the bed is called "Marlow." He knows the girl only as "Hai." His inner consciousness sometimes describes her to itself cinematographically as now, sharply in focus, she bends down straight from the hips stealthily—calves and left buttock small, tight, and bald—the weight of head and torso sensuously stretching the hamstring muscles at the backs of her thighs. The hair, however, stands out almost as a thing in itself. Black and stiffened by lacquer, it juts out from her skull in random twists and spikes. She could be a Greek Fury or a kabuki madwoman.

Marlow-the-watcher closes his eyes and withdraws into himself where he finds that—as he would say—he and the bed smell strongly of sweat and incense, pussy, and perfume. He waits while the girl makes a bundle of her clothing and other belongings and moves quietly into the next room. Meticulous about his few possessions, Marlow tracks the sound of her sandals in various parts of the living room and—when she stops—guesses what she is examining.

A few minutes after her disappearance from the bedroom, the screen door downstairs squeaks. Marlow pushes himself upright and stands to watch as she passes below on the sidewalk that runs along that side of the building. She is carrying a portable radio recently lent to him by a friend. He grimaces, anticipating the energy he will have to expend to get the radio back without hurting her feelings or embarrassing her.

It is early spring in the coastal provincial capital, Vung Tau, located at the end of a peninsula—about a hundred kilometers by road from Ho Chi Minh City ("Saigon" at the time of this story). Vung Tau began centuries ago as a local port and fishing village at the mouth of the river. In the French colonial period, it came to be valued as a rustic seaside getaway for colonial planters and urban bourgeoisie.

It is also the ancestral home of a cluster of powerful Vietnamese families, and because many of those families had converted to Roman Catholicism during the French occupation, the area also was something of a Catholic enclave in this predominantly Buddhist country. When the Americans and their allies needed an in-country "rest and recreation center," Vung Tau was a natural choice. It was relatively easy to defend, and also for several years, its leading Vietnamese families had furnished leaders of puppet governments in Saigon created by colonists—this one American, like the French before them—easing into the preexisting social connections.

At the time of this story, the Catholic families are still influential, and their homes in Vung Tau have come to be places where shadowy men of ambition but diminished influence gather to discuss coups d'état and other forms of political, financial, and military entrepreneurship and skull duggary.

As a rest and recreation center, Vung Tau soon filled up with bars and restaurants, and young peasant women engaged in whatever service activities they could find or invent to take advantage of this new source of revenue. The U.S. Central Intelligence Agency also located training facilities there for some of its paramilitary undertakings and hired *Nung* tribesmen (fabled since ancient times as mercenaries from southern China) as a security force. Thus, Vung Tau—at the time of this story—has something of the feel of a fortified redoubt, an island of artificial tranquility in the midst of a tsunami of violence that has inundated most of the remainder of the country.

Some French families, reluctant to leave the former colony, still come to the village on weekends to camp on the beach. Weaving through all the scurry, posing, and melodrama of the town, children of peasants make their way silently and almost invisibly as best they can.

Alone in the duplex, Marlow is lazily waking and taking inventory of the inside of himself. He imagines something hot to soothe a throat that is dry and sore from smoking too many cigarettes. Peristalsis, he discovers, has continued to work nicely however. Walls of stomach and intestines shift and squeeze a rich mixture—water, metabolites of alcohol, bits of noodle, an occasional peanut hull, pieces of ten-day duck egg (shard of fetal feather, sliver of fetal bone), blobs of sticky rice, aromatic herbs and peppers, a kind of decomposing gruel—all moiling, slowly refracting, liquid siphoning off, nutrients in osmosis, waste accumulating.

Having fallen asleep again, Marlow wakes with a start, sweating into the sheets on the wide, hot bed. A miasma of unfocused guilt coils around him like an indecisive swarm of hornets. He tries to remember if there is something he should be doing. The hour is late. He does not take proper care of his body . . . But it is Sunday. There is nothing to be done, and his body is more or less as he left it.

He rolls onto his back. Some dizziness—no headache. He has dreamed of dismembered people displayed bloody in a butcher's case. He longs for green tea or a piece of fruit to wash away the taste of the blood. He winces at the memory of cannibal gluttony (a fine, bloody haunch, blood coating his fangs and incisors like those of Dracula in love).

He retreats into humor, laughing out loud at himself, but the silent echoes of the guilty fear persist like an unamused audience—gazing without mercy at a desperately untalented comedian. He runs his fingers through his own copper-coil hair, seeking comfort in his robust health.

Not many blocks away, another young American of about the same age—dapper, casual, and cool in preppy chinos, sandals, and a polo shirt—is composing a letter:

> It is Sunday morning now, love, and I will continue this letter (which I fell asleep over last night) by adding another scalp to my cast of characters over here. I have in mind a fellow who is called Marlow. Actually, he says that this nickname was bestowed on him in his college days and has nothing to do with Joseph Conrad. Marlow's story is that he and some friends were hanging out at a dive in Austin, and during the band's break, he stood up and proposed to do his impression of Arlo Guthrie singing what Marlow says was a Merle Haggard standard, "Must You Throw Dirt in My Face?" Some boozed-up customer took offense at this blasphemy, calling Marlow a liar and declaring that Arlo Guthrie had never sung the song; and if he had, he would have sounded much better. Quick-thinking Marlow claims to have saved himself by telling the heckler that he had not said Arlo Guthrie, but Marlow McPherson—whom he described as a wannabe Scottish balladeer—who sang so badly that the only time he sang in public, he was immediately stoned to death and so is not a familiar figure in the United States.
>
> Putatively, Marlow is employed by the International Volunteer Service (IVS), a private version of the Peace Corps, from which organization he receives about $80 per month and other considerations for teaching English to the sons and daughters of Vietnamese businessmen and government clerks. Although it is strictly forbidden that the CIA should hide one of its operatives under that cover, there is really not much that can be done about inviting someone like Marlow to supply this or that bit of information. In fact, many of us suspect that he may indeed have crossed more than one such line. He is just a little too well organized for the kind of bohemian humanist, of which at times he seems almost a parody. There is about him a quiet sense of alertness and precision that can be imagined as sinister, though he claims humorously that self-destruction is his ultimate goal over here. Ironically, the old veteran FBI and army types regard him as a "communist" and regularly warn me ("A bright kid like you, with a career ahead of you") against fraternizing with him.

The distress of waking has dissipated for Marlow. A friend gone to Saigon for the weekend has left him his jeep, which Marlow steers carefully down the street, slightly unaccustomed to driving. He avoids bicycle swarms, motorbikes, miniature buses fabricated on three-wheeled Lambretta motor scooters, and the occasional automobile or ox cart—the last of which are guided by drivers perched on singletree or shaft, steering the animals by goading their giant testicles with bare toes. The buffalo obey impassively.

An old woman, bending under the weight of two full carrying baskets, swinging from her carrying stick, plunges blindly off the curb in front of Marlow's jeep. He slaps down hard on the brake pedal. The front right fender of the jeep stops two inches from the woman. She looks up, startled, then begins to laugh, her mouth a great, dark hole rimmed by betel-blackened teeth. He is frightened momentarily of her black-toothed cackle and imagines what it must be like to kiss her.

That reflection is interrupted by the sharp report of a pistol, loud and close. Instinctively, Marlow ducks then looks around and decides it must have been a firecracker after all. Several people stop on the sidewalk and peer in the direction from which the shot came, before they move on.

Unknown to Marlow, the scene with which he began the new day is unfolding again nearby with minor adjustments. Another girl who will later cross his path (this one named Song) is reaching for something beside a bed. Heat is growing in her small white room. She bends straight from the hips. Her calves and buttocks are tight, hairless. She picks up the bottom half of a bikini. Without straightening, she shakes it out and steps into it. Her torso is parallel to the floor as she pulls the suit up over her hips. She is taller than Hai, who has long since disappeared down Sin Alley. Song is meatier, and her shallow, fat breasts hang down only a little. The bag of guts sags. As she pulls the bathing suit up into place, her long hair hangs straight down in front of her, almost to the floor.

The sharp, short crack of a pistol. Song stops suddenly. Like a wading bird that has sensed the silent approach of a crocodile, she waits intently. Presently, a pair of feet are running in her direction. She steps back from the window, careful not to be marked as a witness.

Meanwhile, Hai rolls over in bed inside a mosquito net. "Hai?" her mother calls from another room. Without opening her eyes, Hai runs her tongue over her teeth and wipes her mouth with the back of her hand.

Unknown to Hai, Song, and Marlow, a young municipal police officer has just shot his wife. Immediately after the shooting, which he found astonishingly easy, the policeman, whom we shall call Tran Ngoc Huong, looked curiously at his wife. She had been knocked back against the concrete wall of their bedroom by the impact of the bullet. As she settled to a sitting position, her eyes were wide. She struggled to move her lips but managed to say nothing.

The front of her pajama top showed a small but growing red spot. Her expression turned to reverie, and she slipped sideways to her left, her torso making almost a dancer's quarter turn. Her head struck the floor with such force that Huong winced. A gray spot of concrete showed on the wall behind where she had been standing. The white paint had been gouged away from the concrete by the exiting bullet. Around a spot of raw, gray concrete, Huong saw a fine sprinkling of red and pink. A wide red smear on the wall marked the curve of her descent to the floor.

Huong stepped forward to look closely at his wife, a Smith and Wesson .38 caliber standard issue service revolver dangling from his right hand. The cloth of her pajama back was shredded around a large exit wound. Roughly a quarter of the back was already soaked red. She was breathing in shudders and appeared to be unconscious. Huong had seen such sights often enough to know that she was dying.

His two children peered in with wide eyes at the bedroom door.

Huong still wore his gray and white civilian police uniform. It was soiled and wrinkled. He swayed, rubbing his eyes. The smell of alcohol filled the room, released by his rapid breathing. He glanced once more at his wife's body, which had grown stubbornly inert in death. He tried to push it out of sight under the bed with the toe of his shoe, but it fell back to its previous position; and rather than struggle with it, he dashed out of the house.

A neighbor woman was looking through a gap in her bamboo fence, trying to see into Huong's open front doorway. As he came out, he pointed the pistol at her. She whooped and scurried away. Jerking out the front of his shirt, he stuck the revolver under his belt as though to hide it. He winced in surprise when the hot barrel touched the bare skin of his belly. Huong rushed through his front gate and headed down the street. The flap of the empty holster slapped loudly as he ran in his pointed black Italian shoes. It did not occur to him immediately to return the pistol to its holster.

Song, having put on pants and a shirt to cover her bathing suit, walks to her window and looks out. The alley is empty except for some children playing quietly several houses down. Almost stealthily, she makes her way out to the dirt street and down past the temple to the white fortress-duplex where she turns left in to Sin Alley, heading toward the house Hai shares with her son and mother.

Unaware of the inexplicable murder that has just played itself out, Marlow steers the jeep along, savoring his mobility. He turns left, heading for the Pacific Hotel. Sunday shoppers in the market area cluster along the street. He sees a disheveled civilian policeman (whom we now know as Officer Huong) running down the sidewalk. Charging past a doctor of astrology, who is hunkered down head-to-head with a client, Huong upends the client and sends the doctor's reference materials sliding and tearing along the concrete walk. The doctor shouts after him. Marlow grins. Simultaneously, he mutters, "The son of a bitch." He instinctively despises policemen.

Reaching the corner, the officer dodges left as a black-suited ancient gray-beard steps out in front of him. The policeman stiff-arms the grandfather in the back and passes from sight around the corner. The old man is propelled into the street, his left hand and the walking stick in his right gyrating above his head. He runs into a slowly moving bicycle. Rebounds. Falls onto his back and lies there—legs, left arm, and walking stick waving. He becomes for Marlow a circus clown, imitating a dying cockroach. Marlow slows to watch the show. He wonders what malefactor the cop could have been pursuing and savors the irony of the disorder caused in the name of law and order, just now sorting itself out in the policeman's wake along the street and sidewalk.

Marlow's amusement abruptly and inexplicably transforms into fear. His jaw stiffens and his hands clamp the steering wheel. His heart slams against his chest. Gritting his teeth until sinews cord his neck, he pulls past the American guard and into the barbed-wire-enclosed parking lot of the Pacific Hotel. He parks, shuts off the motor, and sits in the jeep, waiting for the black panic to recede.

Hai is the second oldest of five children. Like others in the family, her younger brother is ashamed of both her profession and her illegitimate child. Of the family, only her mother has volunteered to live with Hai in town and take care of her young son. Hai has not seen her brother in several months and fears that she will never see him again.

On this particular Sunday morning, the brother, whom we shall call Phuoc, is experiencing something of a crisis of his own. He is lying behind a levee in the same paddy field where his uncle used to allow him, Hai, and their siblings to play in the off season. Phuoc is awakened by the heat of the sun on his back. Dried mud is caked on one side of his face. Ants are crawling inside his jumper. He brushes them away carefully and tries to remove the mud. The sun is almost directly overhead. He would like to walk back to the hamlet, stopping along the way to rinse off the mud and then enjoy a glass of iced coffee with sweet, condensed milk from a can. But his orders are clear: he must remain in place. The old bolt-action carbine that he cradles would quickly betray him in the hamlet. Besides, he is ashamed of having slept through the early dawn. Now the road is too crowded for him to carry out the mission. He brushes crumbs of dirt off the old carbine, admiring the luster of the stock and upper hand guard.

Phuoc is humbled by his good fortune. His cell leader received the rifle two nights ago when one of the liberators came to the village and explained the mission. Phuoc asked his uncle, to whom the cell leader owed a favor, to put in a word for him. Reluctantly, the uncle did as he was asked, and Phuoc was awarded the honor of the mission—and the use of the lovingly preserved old Italian carbine. He worries about his older sister and would like to make himself sufficiently strong to bring her and his mother back to the village and face down anyone who criticized or judged them. He daydreams about being the kind of uncle to Hai's son (whom he has only seen once and then from a distance) that his own uncle has been to him.

Though he is thirsty and his belly is beginning to rumble with hunger, he would not think of leaving his assigned position.

> At twenty-eight, Marlow claims to have given up most things. It is easy to discount that kind of talk as meaningless swagger, but I suspect something is trying very hard to wrench itself free from him—or he from it. He is moody and often surly, but for all his vaunted cynicism and the scathing sarcasm he piles on military and bureaucratic officials for whom he has taken a dislike, I have never seen him speak unkindly to children or to the wretches who live down the alley from him.
>
> He likes to boast that he has been a brick layer, a carpenter, a paratrooper, a trapper of snakes and alligators, and a professional graduate student. With a certain suspension of disbelief, I can imagine him in all those roles. Under the influence of alcohol, he will admit that he once aspired to "Writing" (with a capital W) but hasn't "done anything" for a couple of years. He claims to have broken ties with people at home except his mother, an alligator wrestling uncle for whom he supplied specimens, and the elderly uncle's brilliant and beautiful younger girlfriend. Notwithstanding his fondness for the family (and lust for the uncle's girlfriend), he professes not to care if he never sees the United States again.

Song looks respectable in a modern Western sort of way; the bikini is covered now by the white blouse and black pants. She wears expensive leather sandals and sun glasses. Her long black hair shines, hanging down her back. A matron in the compound at the mouth of Sin Alley scowls at her and pointedly turns away, but Song gives little evidence of noticing, except that her eyes are averted and her forehead momentarily creased.

A block or so along, she passes through a gate that opens onto a miniature courtyard in front of Hai's small house. The house, a lean-to made of unpainted wood and bamboo matting attached to a wall of Marlow's duplex, is distinguished by a brilliant red metal door panel fabricated from Carling's Black Label beer cans—folded out flat and soldered together. The panel flashes red, gold, white, sliver. Its colors are bright and joyful in the dusty front yard. Song gives a friendly nod to Hai's mother, who is sweeping. A small boy plays quietly in a corner of the yard. About two years old, he wears only a shirt. He glances at Song and smiles. She greets him and enters the house and tentatively calls, "Hai?"

Near the end of the peninsula, policeman Huong climbs out of a Lambretta bus that is disgorging its passengers to the beach. To his right, a row of beach bars and restaurants extends to a stark, black rock, which marks the cape by which the area is known. An American soldier and his Vietnamese girlfriend also climb out of the tiny bus and head for the first bar. (Huong spits on the ground in disapproval.)

Huong works his way over two sand dunes to the left of the bar. At each step, he slides backward. Sand pours into his shoes and clings between his toes. Out of sight of people on the beach, he squats to rest and knuckles his pounding eyes. He wishes for a bathing suit and perhaps a woman to escort in order to be less conspicuous. His mind is clearing. He has not been to bed all night and is very tired. He removes the pistol from his belt and replaces it in its holster. He wonders why it was tucked into his pants. He wonders why he killed his wife and how it could have been so easy—and irrevocable.

Marlow, walking across the terrace of the Pacific Hotel officers' mess, amuses himself by pretending to use an imaginary super-cold ray gun to freeze the men sitting in the courtyard on lawn chairs. Inside, he chooses a table, with his mind now on steak and eggs. The imaginary frozen victims of the ray gun he leaves behind to return to life willy-nilly in the heat. In the bar to his right, someone is struggling through a song at the piano.

> With his lumberjack shirts—which he wears in defiance of the heat—and his kinky red hair—which is seldom cut and never combed—Marlow resembles a young Norman Mailer on a book jacket. He would never admit, even to himself, that he does this on purpose. He is articulate and well read, and probably quite intelligent, despite having attended a third tier state university in Texas or Louisiana. When in the mood, he metamorphoses into a lively and stimulating conversationalist.

Marlow orders in Vietnamese from the Vietnamese waitress. They chat. When she leaves, she is smiling, and her slender body has grown straighter.

Rusting grillwork along one wall of the dining room shelters diners from an unnamed menace. Hand grenades or homemade bombs may have come from the outside some years back, but Marlow doubts it. Beyond the grillwork is an enclosed garden, dominated at this time of year by three flowering plants.

Marlow does not know the names of many plants, but one reminds him of magnolia. Another is full of bright little yellow flowers on a tree that resembles mesquite. The third is a gaudy cerise, maybe crepe myrtle, he speculates. Energy from their colors shivers around him in dancing threes. He recalls the names of the Greek Fates—Klotho, who spins the thread of life; Lachesis, who allots its length; and the inevitable Atropos, who cuts it. He almost blushes at his own pretentiousness.

His waitress brings a cup of coffee. Holding it close to his eyes, he surveys the officer's mess from behind a curtain of vapor. At one table, an aging colonel peruses the *Stars and Stripes*. His flabby eyelids hang down like the lids of ancient iguanas. Marlow tries to imagine what might lie behind that dragon visage. Marlow once played against the other man in tennis doubles, but he can't recall the name. A young captain, if he remembers correctly. A pilot. The captain sits now at his solitary table, stoically affecting the hunch and the haircut of a second-string halfback. The three floral gauds in the garden gesture obscenely at Marlow, vying for his attention. He swallows hot coffee.

Song lifts the mosquito net and sits on the edge of Hai's bed. Hai awakens. Her hair stands out all around her face, which under the makeup reveals itself to be slender and pretty. She smiles at Song and, a murmur of friendship runs between them. With studied nonchalance, Hai removes a portable radio from under the pillow and turns it on. Her friend gazes at it covetously but does not mention it.

Marlow hums to himself as he chews. He remembers the old man knocked over. He thinks of Hai, whom he knows mostly as the girl who spent the night with him for the first time last night. Idly, he wonders what her real name is. She was very emaciated, probably tubercular. He slurps at a string of runny albumen and coughs experimentally.

Surreptitiously, he steals a look at his mess mates, neither of whom seems quite real. Nor does his memory of the fallen old man with his waving stick, arm, and legs. Nor the dead of his dreams and accidental encounters. Nor this fucking officers' mess for that matter. *I'm not a fucking officer!* Marlow searches for his wrist to feel the arm hair and the pulse—only to find in the interval between search and clutch (between act and satisfaction) that the very image of his own action confirms the worst: what kind of lunatic holds his own fucking arm just to make sure he is real? The fear this time is suffocating to the point of euphoria.

Another piano player, more enthusiastic than talented, hammers out an Australian song:

> Oh, we're marching to euphoria,
> euphoria, euphoria.
> We're marching to euphoria . . .

Marlow shrugs. The captain and the colonel digest their food while reading *Stars and Stripes*. Marlow has read a copy once. In one section of it were poems sent in by readers. One he remembers went like this:

> My husband has traveled far over the sea
> To fight for the freedom of you and me,
> To fight for our flag with a faith so true,
> To make old Ho his greed to rue.

Marlow and his friends used to laugh a lot at the doggerel and jovially made up obscene parodies. Finally, though, he decided that the poems were not funny, or at least that he was not qualified to laugh. Residue of that feeling has been dogging him for weeks.

Hai and Song stroll along the water's edge, having left their street clothes at one of the beach bars and scampering away from the occasional wave that comes in too far. Hai wears a dark blue bikini with halter cups that are padded on the underside so that her modest breasts bulge at the top. The bathing suit is attractive against her dark skin. Her hair has been brushed and lacquered into a large black bubble. Beside Song, Hai looks especially thin, with her long arms and legs and boyish buttocks, but she seems carefree—walking with loose, free, springing steps and a modest smile on her face.

Groups of American soldiers; small families of French, Vietnamese, and Chinese civilians; innocuous gangs of adolescent boys; and bikini-clad girls like Hai and Song all promenade from the bars, down a mile to the American rest and recreation area and back. The French families established under umbrellas or in tents are, for the most part, the wives and children of plantation managers or businessmen down from Saigon for the weekend.

Officer Huong pops out from behind a sand dune some distance back from the beach and approaches Hai and Song. They look away from him.

"You should not be walking alone on such a nice day," he says, more or less to Hai, his face masked by the formal smile of the supplicant. His shirt tail is out. His clothes are wrinkled and dirty. His trousers are torn at the right knee. He is shorter than either of the women.

"I'm not alone," Hai replies. "I'm with my friend here." Song recognizes the policeman as her neighbor, Officer Huong, and whispers this information to Hai.

"You should walk with me," Officer Huong persists. Hai shakes her head and takes a step away. The formal smile disappears from his face. "Whore!" he cries. "You walk with the common Americans." Not answering, Hai continues to move away from him. He runs to catch up with her and grabs her shoulder to stop her. She knocks his hand away. He looks up at her and thinks of the revolver in its holster, one round expended.

"If you don't leave me alone," Hai says deliberately, "I will tell my friend, Police Captain Chau, and you will be very sorry. I will tell him that you were drunk and insulting and that your uniform looks like you have been sleeping with pigs. In fact, you smell like a pig. He is my very good friend, and I know your name and where you live."

Huong glares at her then disappears back behind the sand dune, like a place daemon or troll. The girls walk on. In Hai's hand, the new radio plays pleasantly. Nearing the American section, the girls turn back. Several soldiers are chasing each other in the surf. They whistle and shout at the girls, who smile back and slow their steps. "Hey, wait a minute," one man calls.

Hai's brother Phuoc listens to the *poc-poc-poc* sound of a helicopter approaching at about five hundred feet along the road he has been watching. The pale gray road runs up the east bank of the river. The helicopter now is turning right, away from the road and heading diagonally across the peninsula. Phuoc thinks of the helicopter as an almost mythical giant eye, which if it sees him will rain down fire and steel. He guesses that now the eye is seeing a jumble of gray-toned greens and browns: muddy water, sparse mangrove in the tidal pools along the water, firewood corded beside the occasional drab house. The eye swings over what Phuoc thinks of as a healthy hamlet, his home. It sweeps the paddy fields, now lying fallow. Phuoc pushes the rifle into bushes and crouches behind the paddy wall where he has been waiting. As though having detected some movement, the eye orbits the field where Phuoc is hiding. Phouc's heart pounds. After a long moment of retained breath, he hears and feels the eye of the helicopter moving on.

> Marlow vociferously opposes our involvement in the war. Consequently, as I said, the retired military types that the AID and the CIA have picked up to fill their personnel vacancies over here consider him a communist and avoid him like the plague. But one is never sure where Marlow stands. Once, when I pointed out to him the obvious fact that even as a noncombatant, he too is contributing to the war effort, he grinned enigmatically, winked, and said, "If you want to play, you got to pay."

Idly, Phuoc fondles the rifle. The helicopter would have been an easy target, but probably he could not have brought it down with one or two shots, and it would have returned fire. Anyway, his cell has been instructed not to shoot at helicopters for the time being. He has already prepared the hole where he will hide the rifle and the American weapon he hopes to capture. Now there is nothing but to wait for darkness to fall again.

Hai and Song have stopped and waited for the American soldiers to catch up with them. Both young women are smiling. They chat briefly before Hai finds an empty beach chair and sits down in it to enjoy the sun, placing the radio under the chair. A small gust of wind blows sand lazily past her. Song and the Americans wade out into the surf and begin playing with a frisbee. Hai cannot join them because of her hair. Just as well. She can now see that they are drinking whiskey, and Song has begun drinking with them. As Hai watches, the Americans begin amusing themselves by swinging Song—one by the wrists and the other by the ankles—and throwing her far out into the water, then openly fondling her when she surfaces.

A short while ago, a Chinese mother from Saigon—whose children were playing near where Hai sits—shooed her children to a spot farther down the beach while scowling at the scene before her. Hai does not blame her. The spectacle jars the serenity of beach and ocean. Hai averts her head pointedly and listens to the new radio.

When she glances out to sea again, Song and the short American are gone. The other American stares, his arms limp. In a moment, the short American comes to the surface. Song does not. The Americans shout and gesture then both disappear under the water rendered murky by the breaking of waves. Hai stands. The Americans reappear. Song does not. The Americans shout, dive, surface, gesticulate, and dive some more. Hai begins to scream. Strangers on the beach run to her. She screams and points. Eventually, the Americans come out of the water, their mouths and eyes hanging open. A woman clasps Hai, and they weep together.

When Song is not found after several minutes, Hai allows herself to be led away to a Lambretta bus up on the road. Suddenly, she breaks free and returns to the beach chair. The new radio is gone. Wailing wretchedly, she makes her way back to the bus.

Awareness has been growing in Marlow that pedestrian traffic on the beach has changed. He lifts his eyes from the book he has been reading. People are moving across his unfocused field of vision. Several GIs stroll as usual, but all the Vietnamese are traveling to his right. Marlow looks down the beach in that direction.

About a quarter of a mile away, a large crowd has formed. He grimaces. Probably a fistfight. He turns back to the book, but no . . . Looking again, he sees the jeep of an acquaintance parked on the sand near the edge of the crowd. Marlow gets out and retrieves his wallet and watch from where they are buried in the sand. Back in the jeep, he starts the motor and drives down to park beside the other jeep.

People in the crowd grin and push. Marlow asks a woman what is going on but doesn't understand her answer. Begging random pardons, he works into the dense center of the crowd. Finally, thrusting aside a couple of adolescent boys, he breaks into an open inner circle.

Song's body lies on its right side, the back to Marlow. She looks heavy. Her nude calves are lumped with muscle, even in repose. The gray-and-white bottom of her bikini has been pulled up into the cleft between the buttocks so that the left buttock is exhibited—fatter than the legs, concave at the side; the skin gray, full of pores even at this distance. The inner ring of spectators are young boys. They grin and ogle. Two Americans in bathing trunks grasp the body by the legs and shoulders and turn it over. The belly is a gray sack of water, distended as though in pregnancy. It sags to the right. A susurrus, sprinkled with giggles, greets her righting. One of the men turns the head to the side, and Marlow can look directly at the face. Her face is familiar, though he can't recall where he has seen her. The mouth is permanently open, curved for a shout or a groan, the mouth of a gargoyle. The eyes are open, dull brown, and filled with sand. The American fishes in the mouth with his finger.

The other man straddles the waist of the corpse and leans forward, pushing down on the chest. The bikini top is up around the neck, exposing small, fat breasts. Though the body looks solid as sandy concrete, the breasts slither under the man's hands and wriggle as he pushes. At the sight, the children shriek, laugh, jostle each other, fall down, get up, imitate the breasts, make faces, and hop about. The man pushes again. The dead breasts dance. The children convulse again. On the third push, foam erupts from the open mouth. A cheer from the children. Push. Relax. Push. Relax. Push. The gargoyle fountain flows.

Marlow looks away, a sense of exhaustion settling upon him. Atropos has cut another thread. He finds an American MP standing nearby and offers the use of his borrowed jeep to take the body to the civilian morgue. The MP shakes his head. "No," he says. "They're going to try mouth-to-mouth."

"But she's *dead,* man!" Marlow cries. "She's *been* dead!" He is embarrassed by the sudden vehemence in his voice. He finds that he wants to weep, although he knows nothing of the woman, or at least nothing that would warrant his weeping for her passing. Even as an organism already microscopically unraveling itself before him and the other spectators—just as he and everyone else will do—it is still something he feels moved to acknowledge or bless. In the end, he decides to do no more than note that he felt like weeping for no reason.

The MP looks past him at the body. "Yeah. Well, we have to try. Then we'll let the Vietnamese handle it. I just got a report that one of the white mice shot his wife this morning and is thought to be heading for here. Looks like a long night shaping up."

Marlow shuts his eyes tightly and opens them, letting go of the pejorative name for the civilian South Vietnamese police with the rest. The man who has been doing manual CPR has finally stopped. The other man kneels by the head. They look at each other. The second man says, "Ready?" The other nods.

Aloud, Marlow says, "I'm not staying for that." He shoves through the crowd. Once clear, he puts his hands on his hips, head down, filling and clearing his lungs. Though he has not worn a football uniform since graduating from high school, the ten-year-old memory of this posture emerges from its resting place in his body—skin on his shoulders shying away from sweat-wet shoulder pads, odors of adhesive tape, lineament, and accumulated sweat.

It was a good feeling then, and the memory of it brings him to safer ground. He looks around for the acquaintance whose jeep is parked nearby. Instead, he sees yet another acquaintance, a young foreign service officer from Saigon. (*Damn. We're like cockroaches around here!* Marlow thinks.) The new man's name is Sam Wetherill. Marlow puts on an appropriately supercilious face, greets Sam, and asks if he is driving the jeep. Sam nods. "Fred Fordham loaned it to me," he says, "and you?" He nods toward the jeep Marlow has been driving.

To get away from the crowd and the dead woman, they walk to a nearby beach bar and order gin and tonic. The two speak brightly to each other, their dialogue animated and stylish, laced with self-conscious cynicism about the war. They follow a formula well practiced by both. (Sam remarks at one point that on a recent trip through the northern provinces, he found the situation "stunningly unchanged.") Pleased to talk and to play the game, Marlow unconsciously expunges his native southwestern Louisiana accent and digs for images that are original, precise, and evocative. Perhaps some of his sayings will be remembered and repeated ("As Marlow McCall said the other day . . .") back in Saigon or in a remote hamlet with others of Sam's kind. Sam treats Marlow like a day guest at his club, gifting him with personal revelations, which, Marlow suspects, are carefully sanitized for his consumption. Sam has recently become engaged (to a flawless and thoroughly vetted debutante Marlow is sure).

Marlow surprises himself by saying that he is thinking of leaving Vietnam. "Yes, I can understand," Sam replies, "the pointlessness of it all. In your job, it must be even worse."

"It's not just that," Marlow says, wondering why he is wasting this much honesty on a Sam Wetherill. "The other day, something happened, and my reality slipped just half a degree, and I slammed right into the ugly realization that when all is said and done, you and I and most of us are just here on a lark while the people whose homes we have invaded are dead—seriously living the only lives they will ever have."

"Well, it *is* your career," Sam begins condescendingly, refusing to be included in Marlow's self-indictment.

"Career?" Marlow practically shouts. "Do you think this kind of stuff is my career?"

Taken aback, Sam temporizes. "Well, not this exactly, of course." Then with just a hint of reproof, he adds, "So what did bring you here?"

"Beats me," Marlow says, lapsing into reverie. At length, he rouses himself. "Probably just didn't want to miss the big show."

Sam laughed. "Well, that's not so terrible, is it? I mean, you are not exactly disgracing yourself."

"That's just it," Marlow adds, nodding to himself, "I am."

Marlow's brain feels like a dam, straining against the weight of poisonous water that has been rising all day. He can almost see the cracks opening and the trickles and rivulets springing into being on the face of it.

"Hey," Sam says, clearly embarrassed by the morbid turn the conversation has taken, "I think that bar girl that drowned down there may be somebody you know." Marlow raises his eyebrows. "Yes, I think she hangs out with that girl Hai that works in the Hollywood Bar. We kept an eye on her for a while. By the way, you need to watch your step with that Hai. She has family in one of the villages up the road who are bad guys."

Marlow tries to imagine Hai as taking any position whatsoever about the war. He wonders if the dead girl really was a friend of hers and realizes that he can't confront her about the radio if she is mourning a friend.

The conversation vanishes with Marlow's silence. Sam looks down at his hands. Marlow glances up, and for the first time, notices smoke rising from a napalm fire on a forested hillside up the peninsula. Three Phantom jets swarm, swoop, and dive like the planes that machine gunned King Kong off the Empire State Building. Marlow is up there with the gorilla, swatting down biplanes. Below them, a bright white strip of beach poses for a postcard. Blue green waves are frozen in their stacked procession toward the pristine shore. Tiny figures of American, Korean, and Australian soldiers on leave; Vietnamese bar girls; and French, Chinese, and Vietnamese families all form an elaborate landscape pieced together for a child's electric train with very realistic-looking decorations.

The toy people stroll and play. A hundred Vietnamese children and youths stand in a circle, laughing at a man blowing into the mouth of a putrefying gargoyle while just outside the circle, two specks—Marlow McCall and Sam Wetherill—lounge in their chairs, gin and tonics in hand like colonial planters, chatting away with wit, civility, intelligence, and charm.

Marlow is reminded of Oscar Wilde's faugh, fey pseudo-insanity during the run-up to the British Empire's demise.

The weakening dam in his brain trembles ominously. Unable to sit still any longer, Marlow mumbles an excuse to Sam, scrambles out of his chair, throws down pilasters to cover his drink, and sprints across to the jeep. Without looking back, he drives away.

At about the same time, Hai has arrived, wailing, at the Hollywood Bar. Her sobbing washes a young boy and the bar's owner up against the wall. An old woman peers in from the back room. A girl of about fourteen slides her smooth cheek along the grandmother's wrinkled arm to have a look. Hai talks incoherently through her sobs, smashes a glass on the floor, spits on the broken glass, and rushes back out the door, taking all the air with her.

The bar is less than a block from the entrance to Sin Alley. Hai walks blindly along the edge of the road. A passing car honks at her, but she does not respond. She passes the house of the American she spent the night with last night. She looks up to see if he is at home and is relieved that the jeep is not there, and no light is on. Miserably, she turns down the alley toward her own home.

> One impediment to a comfortable relationship with Marlow is his utterly opaque freakishness. This afternoon, having run into him on the beach, I walked with him to a nearby beach bar. We were having what I took to be a pleasant chat, though he seemed more touchy than usual about his participation in the war. Then suddenly, his eyes stopped focusing on me. He heaved several deep breaths, muttered something unintelligible, and quit the field—literally jumped up, ran to his jeep, and drove off, "burning rubber" in the sand like a teenager. Just like that!

Marlow drives to his duplex and parks beside the entrance. Instead of going in, he puts on his shirt and trousers, brushes the sand off his feet, and slips his sneakers on, adjusting his feet to the discomfort of the remaining grit. Carrying his book, he heads for the neighboring Hollywood Bar where he sometimes drinks or picks up girls.

Far down the narrow length of the bar—as though at the screen-end of a movie theatre—a young girl bends over straight from the hips, torso parallel with the floor, her black hair hanging straight down in front of her. In her right hand, she holds a short broom with which she is sweeping broken glass into a dustpan. For the first time that day, Marlow does not find it amusing to turn the recurrent scene into something out of an Alain Robbe-Grillet novella.

Marlow's eyes dolly along on top of his body between bar stools on the right, the seats covered by flesh-soft orange plastic; and booths on the left, upholstered in soft red plastic. Inexplicably, he finds the upholstery pleasing. The girl carries the pan of glass shards behind the bar and leans the broom in the corner. Her face is very pretty in profile.

The walls and ceiling are hung with wreathes and streamers that were for Christmas in December, New Years in January, and Tet (the Vietnamese New Year) in February. Now in March, they limply mark nothing but the passage of time. Hearing his approach, the girl faces him then straightens herself. He associates her with the family who own the bar and live upstairs, but he does not know her name. He finds her very fresh and attractive and terribly young for this environment. He is disconcerted that she does not smile at him.

Officer Huong meanwhile is still hiding out behind sand dunes near the beach. He kneels in the sand, burying his uniform. With jerky movements, he checks over his shoulder again and again. The hand that scoops the sand trembles but moves slowly. He does not know how to get off this peninsula without being discovered. Now even the Americans seem to know about him. Lying behind the sand dune all afternoon, he repeatedly considered and rejected what seemed like a pitifully small number of alternatives.

He doubts that the liberation front would have him if they learned he had killed his wife for no reason. The revolver itself might prove to be a bargaining chip, but there would be nothing to prevent them simply taking it from him and killing him. Huong tries not to think of the danger and hardship of the liberators' way of life. Perhaps he could sell the gun and use the money to make his way to Cambodia where his uncle lives, but that is very far. Maybe he could disappear into the slums of Saigon. For a while, he considers Saigon his best chance, although he does not have many friends.

Still undecided, Huong stands and pushes the pistol under the elastic band of his bright red underpants. It immediately slips down the leg of the boxer shorts and to the ground, striking his bare foot. He squats again. His trembling hands scoop the sand off the uniform he has just buried. He shakes out the shirt, carefully rolls up the gun in the gray cloth, and stands to tie the shirt sleeves around his waist. For a moment, he is dizzy from standing too quickly; but as his vision clears in the gathering darkness, he works his way out to the open beach. The crowds are gone, only their shadows remain. Huong tightens the sleeves around his waist. The red underpants, gray in the dusk, flap loosely about his skinny shanks as he hurries toward the water.

Hai's mother has left her alone in the darkening room with the boy. The child, frightened by his mother's weeping, now sits on her lap, snuffling through the aftermath of his own sobs as his mother perches on the edge of the bed. Eventually, she manages to control her own grief and speaks soothingly to the boy. She strokes his small genitals, and little by little, he grows quiet and finally falls asleep.

A shy wind skitters through the alley.

Hai joins her mother in the patio. She tells her about Song's death. Her mother agrees that it has been a terrible day. The mother tells Hai that one of Song's neighbors was killed this morning by her husband, a civilian policeman. Hai sits up straight. "We *saw* him," she says.

Her mother laughs in disbelief.

"No, we really did. Song and I were walking on the beach, and this scruffy-looking policeman came up to us and tried to get us to walk with him. Song told me he was her neighbor. When we refused, he became threatening, but I threatened him back, and he went away."

Her mother looks at her intently for a long time. "Maybe your luck is good after all," she says at last. The two of them lift the bright metal panel, which turns out to be hinged at the top. They prop it open with a pole. A fire burns quietly in a metal barrel, giving off smoke to ward off mosquitoes. As evening deepens, the temperature has fallen slightly, and a cooling breeze dances in from the ocean. Hai sits at a low table and relaxes. A plate of aromatic raw greens and a bowl of boiled fish are on the table. Her mother sits down and fills a small bowl with rice gruel and hands it to Hai. She then serves herself, and the two of them begin to eat.

"The American radio?" her mother asks.

Hai closes her eyes and shakes her head. "Stolen," she whispers.

In the Hollywood Bar, Marlow orders a glass of ice and asks the girl to let him keep the bottle of scotch whiskey while he drinks. She hesitates but complies. He fills and drains the glass twice, as he has seen Gary Cooper do in movies. Filling the glass a third time, he pushes the bottle back toward the girl and hands her a two-hundred-piastre note. She takes the bottle and the money, still without smiling. Sipping his drink, he watches her walk away to the far end of the bar. He calls to the girl in Vietnamese, asking where Hai is.

"No come," she replies in English, glaring at him.

Persisting, he asks in Vietnamese if Hai will be in the bar that evening.

"No come," the girl repeats doggedly.

Marlow does not understand the girl's hostility. Obviously, something has happened.

"Did her friend die at the beach today?" he asks. The girl regards him thoughtfully for a while before nodding solemnly.

He knows that Hai lives in Sin Alley. He does not know about the child or Hai's mother. He discounts Sam's warnings about the family's politics as bureaucratic paranoia. "How unlucky," he says to the girl. On impulse, he gets up from the stool, leaves a good tip, and walks out.

Marlow has been in Sin Alley a couple of times when girls who live there have come pounding on his door in the night, requesting that he intervene with unruly GIs. Many people in the alley know who he is. The first person he comes to points out Hai's house.

An older woman meets him at the entrance to the little yard and asks what he wants. He can see Hai sitting near the fire but politely asks the woman's permission to speak to her. Hai gets up and comes to meet him.

"You are wrong to come to my house," she says without smiling. "My son and my mother live here with me. You have not been invited here. I do not entertain men at my house."

Embarrassment aside, something about what she has said and how she said it gives him the sense of having ventured close to an understanding, which nevertheless continues to elude him. Marlow apologizes sincerely for invading her privacy. He tells her that he saw her friend's body on the beach and has come only to bring condolences. When Hai still does not soften, he suddenly wonders if she believes he has come about the radio.

Impulsively, he says, "Look, I know you borrowed a radio from my house," putting the emphasis on "borrowed." "That's fine. Eventually, I will need it back. It was not mine. It belonged to a friend, but there is no hurry."

She studies him closely. "I saw it at your house," she says finally. "I wanted to take it to the beach. When I was crying about Song, somebody stole it. Maybe I can earn enough to buy your friend another one."

He smiles at her and nods his head. "Too bad we can't replace your friend so easily. Don't think about the radio now, you are sad enough without that."

It is her turn to smile. She invites him to have some tea, and he accepts gratefully. As she goes to put the kettle on the fire however, her mother pulls her aside. "Be very careful," she says. "Do not mention Cac-Lo, especially do not say anything about Phuoc or your uncle. You know how I worry about your brother. You do not know this man or whom he talks to. He has good manners, but he is an American."

Marlow overhears some of this and wonders. Hai returns with a pot and cups. Looking about him, Marlow is moved by the simple domesticity of the two women. Voices of two men erupt in the alley. Their conversation grows loud and rancorous, tearing the quiet of the evening. Marlow rises to see what they are arguing about. He has some difficulty understanding their rural accents.

He takes a step toward the gate, but Hai runs to him. "Please sit down," she whispers urgently. "I do not want you to be seen here." Just then, the boy, apparently awakened by the voices, wanders out of the house and runs to his mother. Hai picks him up and speaks soothingly. As she is carrying him back into the house, the boy sees Marlow over her shoulder. His eyes grow wide, and he loudly asks his mother who Marlow is. She whispers to him, and they disappear back inside the house.

Standing awkwardly in the little courtyard, Marlow looks curiously at the older woman, assuming that she is Hai's mother. Apparently, she has been watching him. She averts her face. Marlow listens to the child's crying grow quieter. In the alley, one of the men admonishes the other not to raise his voice while people are sleeping. Their argument continues more quietly. For a moment, taking away the squalor and the war and the nature of Hai's work, Marlow muses that this feels like somebody's home. He smiles at the naïve arrogance of his thought.

He reflects on the whispered conversation between mother and daughter. Why wouldn't the mother want Hai not to speak of her brother or her uncle or of the village or Cac-Lo? He sits back down and sips his cold tea. The older woman goes into the house, leaving him alone. At last, the argument outside ends, and the men move away. The child is quiet.

When Hai returns, Marlow stands to take his leave. "I'm sorry," he says. "I didn't mean to . . ."

She places a hand on his arm and shakes her head. Quietly, she opens the gate and looks up and down the alley. "Go quickly," she whispers. Marlow walks up the alley, feeling the grit of the beach sand in his shoes.

Officer Huong has floated like a coconut in the current. Shoulder deep in the salty water, he is almost knocked over by a low breaker. He feels the pistol slip out of the shirt. It grazes the back of his leg in its fluttering underwater fall. In the darkness, he gropes for the rounded steel with his feet. He tries to dive to find it, but he does not know how to swim. It is gone. Without the pistol, he has lost his last hope of raising money to escape, not to mention the possibility of using the weapon for protection or crime.

Doggedly, Officer Huong remains neck deep in the South China Sea. He hopes that now that it is dark, the tide will change, and the current will carry him toward the sparsely settled upper part of the peninsula. Almost naked and unable to swim, he bobs. He waits for the tide to change. He thinks no further. He knows nothing at all about tides. He fears sharks and crabs. He tries relaxing and allowing himself to drift. He tries to meditate.

In an hour, the miserable policeman has drifted back down to where he started, near the now-darkened beach bars. Trembling violently, he wades out of the water, sits on the sand in the moonlight, and weeps.

Sam continues,

> I suppose that we all have our little eccentricities. Otherwise, we wouldn't be here in the first place, but nobody bears his strangeness as proudly as Marlow does. For example, he has developed the unhealthy habit of riding around the countryside unarmed at night whenever he can borrow a jeep. I asked him once if he believed that he would be safe because he had not overtly harmed the enemy. Affronted, he looked at me in surprise and replied, "Of course not! Surely you don't think I'm that naïve, do you? I came here to die." So much for Marlow, sweetheart. He may not be with us for long, and if he is not careful, I will have to report him to the embassy for his own protection as well as everyone else's. Happily, he confided to me tonight that he has decided to resign his job. That of course, looks to be the best solution for all.
>
> Good night, my love. It won't be long.

Phuoc crawls up onto the dyke, the rifle in front of him. With the coming of darkness, traffic on the highway has thinned to a trickle. He adjusts his position until he has a clear view of the highway for a hundred yards and can see other bits of it further to the east. He breathes deeply to steady himself and waits.

Marlow has come to life again once he is back in his apartment. This has happened often in the past, but it has never lasted. Marlow never mentions this to anyone, nor would he expect anyone to believe it any more than he believes it himself for that matter. Nevertheless, at some level, he feels quite certain that he dies; and that each time, he lives again, recalling the terror of the one and the pain of the other. He remembers a few weeks ago, spinning himself around on the barstool, creating a kind of whirlpool in his mind. At the mouth of the whirlpool, flotsam of past "lives" raced in a circle, randomly emerging as ephemeral webs of detritus that quickly disentwined and trailed on independently.

Something is different this time though. He is tempted to identify the new emotion as shame, but of what, he does not know; and there is far less dissociation. For the first time in a while, he feels tightly bound by what he thinks of as reality. Still, there is the shame. He can think of nothing particularly shameful about his behavior. Yet the feeling remains that "coming back to life" this time has not been welcome. He showers the sand and salt off himself, hoping that the change will melt the shame. When it doesn't, he pours himself a tumbler of scotch and drinks half of it down. Then he dresses in fresh clothes. The unpleasant feeling has not abated, though the alcohol's warmth is welcome in his belly. He finishes the whiskey as he puts on dry sandals, hoping a ride will clarify his feelings.

In a few days, Sam's fiancé will read,

And so much for this letter too, my love. I have to catch a plane to Saigon in the morning. I miss you, and of course, not everything is terribly pleasant here. (Is it anywhere?) But three more months is not unendurable, and after that, all this will be a memory for us.

The wind is bracing as always. Marlow drives with his headlights off, enjoying the soft dampness of the air. He slows going through Rac-Dua and turns on the headlights. He decides to leave them on. From the thatched bars along the road, villagers watch him pass. The moon is bloated orange.

Hai has told her mother that she will walk back to the bar to see what plans are being made for Song's funeral. At the entrance, she sees two Americans sitting in one of the booths. The girl the Americans know as Jenny is just placing bottles of beer in front of the men, and as she turns to leave, one of them pats her slender hips. She looks up at Hai and makes a face. Drawing in her breath, Hai straightens herself and saunters up to the booth where the men are sitting. She lays an arm across the shoulders of the nearest one and says, "Hello, you." The man moves over, and Hai sits demurely beside him.

In the meantime, Phuoc has gotten to his knees on the dyke under the fat moon. On the beach, at the tip of the peninsula, Policeman Huong has dug up his trousers and is walking barefoot down the road into town. He has decided to go to the home of a man he knows to be involved with the armed liberation forces to see if he can arrange to be accepted into their ranks. He does not look forward to living their hard life. He will not see his wife again anyway. He misses her for the first time in his life. Phuoc thinks of his sister and nephew and wonders when he will have a chance to see them again.

For the headlights of Marlow's jeep, bamboo fences make a momentary corridor, then he is out again in the open salt marshes. With the faint thrill of invited danger and the cool young air, he feels the alcohol retreat from his brain. He decides that he will turn around at Cac-Lo. So much for riding all night. Briefly, he remembers that this is Hai's home village and that her brother still lives there. He wonders why it was important that Hai did not mention any of that to him. At the low bridge over the salt water slough, he slows again. The Popular Forces guard is asleep on one of the railings. Marlow honks the horn, shouts, and bellows laughter as the startled man falls off the railing.

Phuoc sees headlights. He lifts the old rifle, glad that it is a carbine and easy to lift. The car is a sedan, probably French. He lowers the rifle again.

Marlow tenses as his lights pick up a group of teenagers sitting in the middle of the road, but they make way for him, calling insults and laughing as he goes. He passes on, past the naval base, and out into open fields again.

Sitting on the dyke in his uncle's paddy field, two kilometers this side of Cac-Lo, Phuoc sees another pair of lights then hears the whine of a jeep being driven fast. He raises the lovingly maintained old rifle. Not having eaten in two days, he feels weak. The rifle wavers. Moonlight glints off the hand-rubbed wood. He steadies it. The jeep rushes to him. He can just make out the front sight of the rifle and looks beyond it with both eyes for night vision.

Approximate. He points the beautiful carbine at the center of the jeep and swings the muzzle one jeep length to the right—going very fast, two lengths ahead. He fires.

A terrific rap on the jeep's windshield. Glass flies over Marlow. Surprised, he jerks the wheel to the right. The jeep skids sideways. He overcompensates and skids back. The right rear wheel hits the roadside ditch and pulls the rest of the jeep after it into the mud.

A freight of fear engulfs him—the thing so often imagined, so inescapably at hand. The jeep has come to a sudden stop. He has hit his head. Something jolts and burns just under his chin. A loud, startling report follows immediately. "Shit!" Marlow dives to the pavement and scuttles across into the far ditch. He parallels the road for a few yards on knees and elbows. The fear has evaporated in the heat of necessity. He hears the *snick-snick* of a round being chambered in a bolt-action rifle. Another shot. Back at the jeep, glass tinkles. Marlow crawls through mud to two large bushes, wedges himself between them, and then pushes through to the other side.

Well, this is what you said you wanted.
So what are you doing now?

Nobody is in the jeep. The realization is like a blow to the chest. Phuoc rushes to the front of the vehicle (TN plates—American) and kicks out the other headlight, temporarily glare blinding himself. He crouches, waiting for his vision to return. Why has the American not returned his fire? Surely the man has a weapon. Otherwise, the entire mission is wasted. Phuoc looks up and down the ditch the jeep is mired in but sees nothing in the bright moonlight. Standing, he moves in a crouch toward the far ditch, expecting to draw fire.

Marlow has wriggled his body around until he can see the road. He rubs mud on his face to darken it. He watches the crouching sniper's head, neck, shoulders, then torso and legs come into view. He loses him as he steps down into Marlow's ditch. With the silhouette of the man gone, Marlow listens to the soft pad of footfalls muffled by mud. Burning under the chin—either a bullet or a shard of glass. On his cheek, cool, sweet-smelling mud—rich in germs.

Phuoc is quaking. He must run away soon. The full moon spotlights him. He must leave before another car comes. But he remains empty-handed. The thought of failure after his uncle has worked so hard to get him this opportunity is horrifying. The shame would be unbearable. He stands up straight as he walks past where Marlow is hiding, hoping to lure the American driver into the open. He stops to look around. The wind holds its breath.

Marlow inhales deeply but silently, drawing up into his shoulders all the weight and ferocity he can amass—and lunges. With the sides of both fists, he chops down the narrow shoulders before him—near the neck—aiming for the double blow to stop halfway down the delicate ribcage.

The carbine slaps against the muck. Phuoc's right arm is not responding. Desperately, he twists sideways and onto his back, trying to wrench himself free. Marlow slips in the mud but manages to fall with his heaviness on top of the boy. How thin their necks are! Marlow's thumbs are under the larynx—probing, penetrating, seeking to crush it. Phuoc gargles, the legs thrash, then he lies still, becoming an "it."

Finishing his letter to his fiancé, Sam tells, her,

Write me long letters, darling. They keep me sane and clean. And know that I love you. Good night.

Marlow reaches over for the rifle where it lies in the mud. *It is an old one, Carcano, made by the Italians for the Japanese.* His mind takes flight into trivia. The body lies as small and distorted as a dropped doll. Using the carbine as a walking stick, Marlow levers himself up to the highway. The jeep is mired to the axles. Marlow balances the carbine in his hand. His head is preternaturally clear. Something more than himself—either alien or heretofore unrecognized—is in him. He feels a burning rush of energy, but at the same time, another part of him has stepped back to watch—curiously.

Not to remember would be sacrilege. Marlow lifts the weapon, he cradles the stock in the crook of his shoulder and works the bolt. An empty cartridge is ejected and flies out to his right. He pushes the bolt forward, and the next cartridge in the clip slides smoothly up and into the empty breach, leaving the weapon loaded. He locks the bolt down but does not put on the safety. He runs his hand up the smoothness of the upper hand guard to the barrel. It is still warm from the shots that were fired. Rubbing the pad of his thumb over the pads of his fingers, he feels the slightest film of oil. He sniffs the fingers—bore oil and burned propellant.

He stands for a moment, head down, entranced. Feeling the lightness of the weapon, he visualizes pushing the muzzle up under his chin, using his thumb to work the trigger. "Easy." Finally rousing himself, he shakes his head. He draws a lungful of air, savors it, and releases it.

As though a giant projector has been started up again, Marlow returns to life yet again. He grasps the barrel of the rifle in both hands, rocks back and forth like an athlete about to throw an Olympic hammer, and swings the shining relic up and out to sail end over end far out over the paddy field, moonlight marking its flight. The chambered round explodes on impact with a startling noise and a flash of light. The soft, sodden sound of the rifle's landing blends with the sharp report.

Hands on hips, Marlow looks toward where the rifle disappeared. He turns deliberately and bestows a final glance upon the innocence of the grotesque little body. He experiences a kind of connection with the unfathomable mystery of vanished life. How could it ever have existed? A current runs up into him from the corpse, a cold heaviness and a growing physical memory of the awkwardness of the posture death has left behind. There is no grace, no poetry, no adventure, no redemption, no guilt that is not hypocritical or self-aggrandizing—just this ungainly mess. He smells shit. The kid's bowels have voided. Nature's efficiency.

Marlow climbs into the mired jeep, sweeps the broken glass out of the seat, and gets the motor running. Hoping for the best, he shifts into four-wheel drive and rocks the vehicle back and forth until it climbs sightlessly back up onto the road. Under the full moon, the absence of headlights is not a serious problem. There is little or no traffic at this time of night. Marlow keeps his eyes on the oil pressure, temperature, and fuel gauges; but nothing vital seems to have been hit.

He drives slowly, only to see by moonlight what he may have overlooked on the way out when he was riding in the blindness of headlights. It also gives him time to reregulate himself. He will have to tell Hai's mother, who he assumes is also the boy's mother. No need to confront Hai. He can afford to buy a replacement radio for his friend. His days at the Hollywood Bar are over anyway. He expects to be out of the country in a week at the most.

In his belly, he already feels what will be the long memory of the boy's death inside him. But for the moment, he feels equal to that burden. And at the same time, he senses another host of imaginary burdens he now can lay down.

As usual, he can't imagine why it took him so long to learn that.

For now, there is only this: the spoiled body of a boy in a ditch back down the road, another body of a harmless girl from the beach, now safely body bagged, with her fat little breasts and big belly, sea foam dried on her cheeks, and sand in her eyes.

The children have had their laugh by now. Laughing is probably as good as anything, but Marlow remains dissatisfied. He pulls the jeep over to the roadside and, by moonlight, scribbles on a folded sheet of paper and puts it into his shirt pocket so that he can examine it later to see if it was worth keeping.

Edwards Brothers Malloy
Thorofare, NJ USA
April 30, 2013